D1558747

"*River Runs Red* is a cunning mix of lyricism and grit. A triumphant and beautifully written historical novel."

JOE OKONKWO, AUTHOR OF *JAZZ MOON*

"Scott Alexander Hess crafts another memorable, beautifully written tale. Gritty and dark. Unrepentant. Vivid. The Mississippi River is the murky yet magnetic centrepiece throughout. 5 Stars (out of 5)."

ONTOPDOWNUNDER REVIEWS

"The opening scene of Scott Alexander Hess's new novel, River Runs Red, is equally powerful and uncomfortable: Orphan-turned-derelict Calhoun McBride, living in 1891 St. Louis, turns tricks on the banks of the Mississippi River, the fictitious Snopes Brewery standing in the distance. Soon, he'll meet Clement Cartwright, the ambitious architect who designed a skyscraper—the world's first—called the Landsworth Building. Their introduction will set off a scandal in St. Louis that culminates in a court trial in the book's final chapters."

ST. LOUIS MAGAZINE

"Hess is artful...McBride's lengthy set-piece trial for attempted murder is fully realized, making points about class, race, sexuality, and greed."

PUBLISHERS WEEKLY

ALSO BY

SCOTT ALEXANDER HESS

*Diary of a Sex Addict*

*Bergdorf Boys*

*The Butcher's Sons*

*Skyscraper*

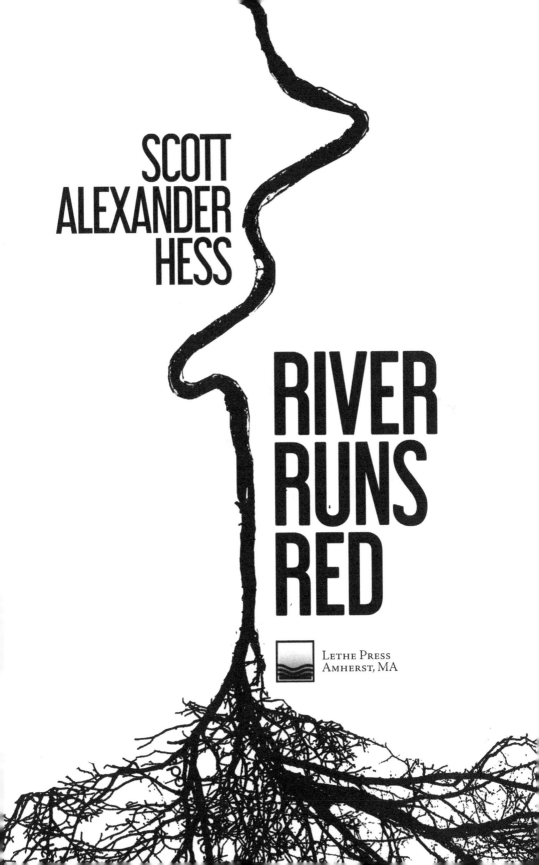

SCOTT
ALEXANDER
HESS

RIVER
RUNS
RED

LETHE PRESS
AMHERST, MA

Published by Lethe Press
lethepressbooks.com

Copyright © 2019 Scott Alexander Hess

ISBN: 9781590217122

No part of this work may be reproduced or utilized in any form or
by any means, electronic or mechanical, including photocopying,
microfilm, and recording, or by any information storage and retrieval
system, without permission in writing from the Author or Publisher.

Library of Congress Cataloging-in-Publication Data
available on request

Cover and Interior design
by Inkspiral Design

*For* FRANKLIN LEARY

PART ONE

# ONE

*Calhoun at the river. Thirteen dollars. Waiting for Fat Frank.*

*Calhoun McBride*

AT NIGHT, THE Mississippi River is mean and ain't quiet. Dark waves smack the cobblestone shore and lick my dirty feet. My pants are roped round my ankles. My drawers, too, but I ain't bothered to yank 'em up. It's too damn hot. July's been steaming so far. Might just kick them off and take a swim. My ass got scraped from the tall fella grinding on top of me before I flipped onto my belly and we got to the real deal. I need a good wash. It's after midnight and Fat Frank's due any minute. Steamboats three deep butt the levee, stretching half a mile, stacked sky high with cotton bales.

Tonight's money was skittish, a lanky man pretty drunk and flush with dollars, likely on his way to Chicago. Maybe a preacher since he paid me before and hurried off scared, checking the sky like some almighty was gonna scorch him. Shoulda made him take me back to his hotel, but sometimes they pass out too fast. Best to get them off right away. He was rough, and pretty darn loud, which is risky outdoors even by the river's edge. But I'm a dollar closer to buying a train ticket to a wide-open country, a sky where stars ain't choked with smokestacks. Over my shoulder I see the Snopes brewery belching black. It never stops, a good thing since the night shifts take on us river boys. Hauling and tossing. Saved me from freezing on the street my first winter in St. Louis. A nickel an hour ain't bad.

Muddy water laps over and over, lulls me, pulls me back three years to the half dream that won't die. I can still see the grave-shallow eyes of the smallest ones. The dirty faces pressed close and tired. I can still hear the soft hum of train wheels moving fast over moon-oiled tracks, all of us huddled and stinky, shoulder to shoulder, hungry cargo from New York heading to Missouri or Illinois or Ohio on the Orphan Train.

I was thirteen, making out just fine in the dark corners of New York when the damned do-gooders shucked me up, forced me on that train. They told us kids that a Mr. Charles Brace was gonna save us all. Some beak-nosed lady in black got us in line, said the Children's Aid Society was gonna cure the orphan epidemic; clean the streets of the dirty left-overs that the churches and orphanages had no room for. Save the wild orphans, urchins, all of us.

I think a few hundred got shipped off to a better life, a real home. But not me. First night on that train, an old drunk snuck on for a free ride, sat upright in a corner guzzling flame fuel, spooking us kids and singing in a crazy voice: "Orphan train running, running. Ain't no getting off. Better not shut your eyes, gonna lose ya in the dark."

Mean old cuss with bright eyes and bright red face staring at me like I was supper. They threw him off next stop at the edge of Pennsylvania, but the little ones kept crying and his liquor stink, his slow dying, and that song stuck on me. I heard tell that farmers were gonna reach in and check my teeth like a horse. See if I could stand long hours of work, live on little food.

"Ain't nobody shoving a fist in my mouth," I told the scrawny boy next to me who was gray-faced with the whooping cough.

I decided then and there I'd get off that train, get away, and I did. I hopped off next morning and ran fast, got away from that ragged litter, thinking I'd find Chicago. But this river took me over, drew me close and I ended up in St. Louis, a city as fine as any in the nation.

It ain't been so bad. First week ratting around the riverfront half-starved I met Fat Frank, the best damn friend a fella could ask for. He taught me night fishing, card playing, and how to survive on the river's edges, staying clear of the mighty steamboats and money men, living in the black shadow of city life. First time he got me out of a bad scrape—before he gave me a place to sleep in his shack, before I knew what he'd become to me—we was at a poker game down in Soulard. It was a rotten, blood-shot crowd, but winter was on hard and anything out of the snow suited me. I played it fair and won big, but one old cuss had a knife, flung it high over his head, wailing and ready to carve me up. He had wild white hair and a scar that ran from lip to ear. He fell on me and the blade cut into my chin, feeling like it would slide past jaw, like it might move slick into and then out the other side of my throat. I tasted blood and saw fire before Fat Frank grabbed a hunk of that greasy white hair and threw him against the wall. Left a scar of crimson there, that dirty old cuss crying. That was the first time Fat Frank saved me. It ain't been the last.

He's the one thing I'm gonna miss when I leave but I'm nearly sixteen and it's high time I get on with life. I had enough of this city's bloody underbelly. I've cheated a few too many times at poker, wandered too many sad back alleys, worked too many midnight shifts at the Snopes brewery.

I'm heading west. Wyoming. Out where a man can see sky and stars. I got exactly twelve of the twenty-five dollars toward my ticket on the transcontinental railroad. I wish Fat Frank would go with me, but he's old and ain't ever leaving this city. Plus he got his lady, the love of his life, crazy Bessie.

Over the hard roll of all that thick brown water I hear something sweet, a cool night calling. It's a lady singing on the Memphis Belle riverboat coming toward shore. Some actress entertaining the fancies. Her voice a call through the blackness. The boat slows to a stop in the distance, a real beauty. White washed clean and painted bright, shouting its name in big red letters stretching from bow to stern.

Midnight moon slashes through the clouds spilling over the mud-stink river. There's death and life sunk down there. I can see that, taste that when I dive deep at night, eyes wide open through the muck and mud, feeling the heat of it in summer staring up through the water to catch the moon like a round white bone smeared with dirt. The Memphis Belle is moving again, slipping by real slow. The singer lady has gone quiet.

What will the night sounds be like out West?

# TWO

*The architect comes home. Memories. A grand building.*

*Clement Cartwright*

SLIPPING INTO THE city at midnight I feel like a bandit. I'm a Chicago man but St. Louis will always be that bright place of beginning, my most steady stretch of youthful unrest that led me past dreams of being a street boxer and onto building things.

From the deck of the Memphis Belle riverboat, I can see her in the distance, past a sleepy cast of steamboats piled with cotton, the city of my boyhood, all shadows and scattered memories. I'm alone on deck. From inside this monstrous tub (a hundred feet long with a four-story paddlewheel) a gal named Delilah is singing, her voice loud and clear over the splash of the slow-churning Mississippi.

My folks are long dead and I have no kin to welcome me. It would have been smart to take the railroad during daylight, get right into the rush and bustle, stopping for a beer in Clabber Alley or Wildcat Chute, my first rough stomping grounds. But there's something about traveling on water that's always soothed me. Maybe because I swam this river so much as a boy.

I'll take a stroll around town today before going to the Landsworth building, the Planter's House Hotel, the home of Mr. and Mrs. Charles Brattridge for a dinner party in my honor with a room stuffed with swells.

I haven't slept and have had a few whiskeys. The boat stopped but is moving again, inching toward the shore crowded with sleepy steamboats three deep. It's a clear night and the stars hover pale and trembling above a thick coverlet of smog, which thickens with the ever-belching smokestacks of Snopes Brewery and a score of other industrial bullies that crowded in since my time here.

It's a grand looking city, past the steamboats and late-night stragglers on shore, buildings rise both high and low stretching densely inward from the river. The Landsworth will reach higher than any other here, the world's first skyscraper according to the *New York Bugle*. My building, my passion, my destiny. Though, according to the city's richest man, Belasco Snopes, I am nothing more than an uppity Chicago architect, an unwelcome outsider who does not belong in St. Louis.

As we near I see a figure, walking toward the levee edge, alone, and for a moment it appears as if he is lifting an arm to wave me in but I know it's only my weariness, the rock of the boat, the drift of the smog, the shadows long lost of this city that sent me off at seventeen to find my destiny. Still, as we inch ever closer, and that figure turns away, I have an urge to shout to him. I summon a memory of my father waving me in from a late-night swim, not waiting for me to holler back, just moving away so he can get ready for a night shift at the brewery. I don't think of him much. I don't think of anything much other than work. The Landsworth Building, the constant chaos of our Chicago projects, our planned work here on the St. Nicholas Hotel. It leaves me sleepless, it never ceases though I can't help wonder what my father would say as I return the much-heralded architect. He hadn't objected to my ambitions, or to me leaving town. My mother had said it was a blessing that I gave up boxing.

As we dock, the singer's gone quiet. Just beyond the river's churn, I can hear the soft lull of restless cicadas. I turn back to the river, throwing my hand up high as if scattering star-shaped ashes of things that were.

# THREE

Fat Frank arrives. Train ticket. Bessie's plan.

*Calhoun McBride*

I SEE A big shadow in the distance. Fat Frank coming 'round the bend down at river's edge. In the dark, him so black, looks like a shape coming to life, like some old charcoal drawing the devil decided to sketch in the mist. He's a big man, tall and carrying all that girth, but he's got a smooth head like a baby's and sad, gentle eyes. There's a scar looks like the sliced off wing of a bird on his right cheek. He never told me how he got it. He's dragging his bad foot, yanking it forward hard but gentle, like it was a bag of gold, and I hear his song. Fat Frank's always singing, humming some old gospel song nobody ever heard of, in that dark voice of his, rich, deep and rushing like the river itself. He's getting closer and I see that bad foot, hear that crazy song from heaven. He holds up a few feet away and starts to laugh. That's the other thing about Fat Frank, always laughing. Whether somebody just died or got born, he laughs long and loud. He says laughing keeps him sane through things too dark to repeat, things that happened before the War Between the States.

He nods at my bottle. "What you got there?" He comes closer, and I lift up the rye.

"You fixing to share? You gonna show pity on a thirsty old man," he says.

"You ain't old."

"But sure am thirsty," he bellows, and then rips into a dark, low laugh.

He keeps that laugh going all the way through coming to my side, maneuvering his girth slowly down onto the cold, wet cobblestones, heaving and sighing, stinking as always like wet leaves and tobacco, taking the bottle from me for a good long snort.

"So, what's good?" he asks after his second nip, handing the rye my way.

He always starts like that. What's good? Me fixing to jump right in with how this one screwed me and that one's after me. He makes it hard to talk shit, that Fat Frank.

"Weather's good. Heat broke," I say, drinking.

"Yup." He drinks again, then goes back wide on his haunches, settling the mass of himself onto the cobblestones like he was settling into a comfortable old chair. Fat Frank makes the best of most situations.

"I got something to tell ya, Frank," I say.

A paddleboat whistle shrieks from far off. It blows again and we both take in the sky. A million pins of silver.

"How you think they ever got them stars to fit up there?"

I grumble a little, take another snort. I know he heard me. "I don't know."

Low, soft laugh. Another snort. "You always in a rush ain't ya, but then you young."

I steal a glance at him, the bulk of that man staring up at the stars smiling, and I think he's like a big gentle bear, and I think he already knows what I'm gonna say, he already knows I'm going away and my jaw tightens up and I'm feeling too tight in my throat to say a word because I'm afraid now, afraid to leave Fat Frank, knowing that he's the only man I ever really felt any closeness to. He laughs low and light and it all smooths out. It's always that way with Fat Frank. He's got magic.

"When you going?"

Through the night, again comes the sound of that paddleboat whistle far off. "Not sure," I say. "Gotta make some traveling money. Then I'm going west."

"How much ya got," he says.

"Got twelve dollars. Need thirteen more."

"Work more night shifts at the brewery," he says. "Less you too spooked." He laughs low.

"That's Bessie's doing. Telling me them tall tales," I say.

First time I got night work at the Snopes Brewery, I told Fat Frank and Bessie and right off Bessie starts filling my head with stories about how the place is cursed, about how old Mr. Snopes Sr. hung himself from a ceiling beam down in the caves where they store the lager, how he wanders looking for boys to drown in the beer barrels. Course my damn luck, first night on they ran me down to the cave, down to that cool under-place that stretches for five blocks below the factory all the way to the shipping yards by the river. It was quiet, dark and damp. I thought I was alone. Then I heard something scraping across the stone floor, like claws on metal. Something was prowling around and I thought it had to be a possum or river rat. The scraping got louder, slow and steady, and I saw a figure in the distance carrying a lamp, mean fingers of shadow cutting ahead of him, spider like, as if the shadows themselves could reach out and grab me by the throat. He crept closer and I saw it was Belasco Snopes Jr., the owner. He was pale wearing a black suit and boots with spurs that scraped behind him. He came up close to me and lifted his head like he was sniffing the air.

"I smell a dirty drab," he said. "Get to work you dirty drab." He disappeared into blackness.

I shiver now just thinking about it. I pass the rye back to Fat Frank.

"Them caves would spook any man," I say.

"Aw shit," Frank says.

I think that's aimed at me, but I see coming our way, like my remembering summoned her, is Frank's own Bessie. She's moving slow; tall and tight, hair all ratted and tied up under a hat with a feather. She's wearing some crazy black get-up with striped stockings and a heel that makes her go real cautious across the cobblestones. If she weren't crazy she'd scare me.

"Here comes my light," he says, the words soft like a bird's coo.

Everybody knows he'd kill for Bessie. She starts yelling. "Goddamn, what you doing down here, making it like this for me, Frank!"

She's going on about the cobblestones, tripping toward us in them shoes. Fat Frank lets out a roar, and his laugh catches into her and she starts ripping up, too, laughing so hard she falls smack on her ass, then has to half crawl before she can re-launch the whole operation and make her way to us. She finally sits by Frank, pecking him a couple times hard on the cheek, laughing and cussing then grabbing the bottle.

"Well what a night baby, what a night," she says between gulps of the rye. "Somebody got us something good. None of that Jimmy rock gut. Who got married? Did baby fall in love?"

I stopped telling her not to call me baby a while back. Waste of time. "I'm heading west."

They both stay quiet. We all stare at the starred-up night sky and listen to the river. I wish the singer's voice from that boat would come back, a low sad song to comfort me. But it stays quiet. Not even a night wind.

"I gotta find a way to make thirteen dollars."

Frank lets out a slow hiss from his near shut lips.

"Well shit," Bessie says. She's up on her haunches coming at me, crawling, and I ain't quick enough plus the rye has lulled me, so she's on top of me, straddling, all that long fancy blackness hanging over me. "A fine-looking thing ain't got to try too hard, you know that. Bessie can get you all tied up fast. All that pretty dark hair and you all soft and white like that. Shit. Ladies like what you got baby. Bessie knows."

She once spied Fat Frank and me skinny-dipping in the river late night. Even under the moon she got a good clear look, hooting and hollering. She chased me around making me feel like some fool.

"He don't want any more of that," Fat Frank says. "He's gonna find his way into something good."

"Hold on there. Don't say what I don't want."

I know what Bessie trades in. She knows men and even some women, some mighty important people, with all kinds of secret needs. She once told us about a fella that dressed up in a bear suit and fed some rich fellow pears all night long. That was it. Made real good money doing that. Bessie has her hands on her hips now, and I see she got her face done up pretty tonight. A deep smear of red on each cheek. Flaming lips.

"What you got in mind?" I say. "I ain't talking chicken shit."

She rolls off me and rolls right over to Frank, who grabs her close. She sighs like she's thinking, then turns back to me. "That new Landsworth building set to open. Whole lot of rich new folks in town. There's a big party happening over on Vandeventer tomorrow night that wants help if you can clean up half good and work in a kitchen."

"What money can I make slopping pots?"

She laughs real low. "Big man don't want to get his hands dirty. You think you can do better without Bessie, go on. You'd be surprised what you might find in a house like that. Secrets in every corner."

I know Bessie set up some dirty things up for some real important people. She deals in things nobody else wants to even think of, and that's where the money is. Plus, anything's better than the night shift at the brewery.

"All right."

Frank does another hiss through his teeth, then passes me back the bottle and starts to sing softly, and I think about how bad I'm gonna miss him. We three lay side by side by side, nothing but the fading beat of the river's waves, and Fat Frank now, making music as the night wears on.

# FOUR

*Seaman's knots. Memories of Daddy. The trouble with Belinda.*

*Belasco Snopes*

THERE ARE HUNDREDS of intricate and binding seaman's knots. The square, the lark's head, the clove hitch, the cat's paw. The bowline was my first knot as a boy, and is most like a noose. Make a small loop, and then pass the end of the rope through the loop. So simple. Daddy taught me that and other knots, one long, hot afternoon when I was eight. It was the day he explained the responsibility, the glory, and brilliance of being a Snopes. It was the day he warned me about the filthy drabs.

I'm nude in my bed, a massive Victorian four poster hoisted four feet off the floor, piled with throws of mink, chinchilla, fox and leopard nearly swallowing me. Only my hands and head are not submerged. I've always imagined my bed as a ship, floating high and powerful.

In my lap I hold a three-foot length of basic manila rope, a pale faded brown, worn and fringed at its edges. I'm fussing with the halyard bend knot, a coy and complex overlapper that tantalizes me in its complexity. I wear thin, very tight calf gloves to save my hands from chaffing.

Playing with the rope soothes my ragged nerves. The idiocy of the upcoming Brattridge affair has me completely untethered. Honoring Clement Cartwright, the Chicago traitor. Blasphemy. It sets my teeth on edge. I stroke the rope, constructing brick by brick a case to destroy Cartwright. I had a steaming bath, a cocaine ankle shot. That helped, but I will need to get out tonight, to soothe this disgust over having to mingle with mediocre men. I will go to the river front later and find my dirty little Jenny Claire.

My bedroom, which takes up half of the third floor of our home on Deminil, is windowless (I had those bricked up). A long narrow hallway, which Daddy agreed to construct for my fifteenth birthday, cuts into the side of the room from the staircase landing. Visitors enter in blackness, fumbling, often calling out, and having to traverse the hall before they enter my bedroom proper. I am never caught off guard.

Once entering, they face a chaotic situation of furnishings. Soaring sculptures on the floor and on teetering tables of mahogany and granite. A byzantine pew, a rustic altar, five standing mirrors all from Rome. Every inch of wall is jammed with paintings. The crucifixion, peasants at work, the fox hunt, slaughtered things, nymphs, subtle lovemaking in garish and bright oils covered with a sheathe of silk. "He who enters is changed." Daddy understood and applauded my undertaking. He smiles now from his mausoleum.

Belinda, who I know has entered and is hovering and trembling in the hallway, detests this room. Since Daddy's death, she is forced to ask me for money or anything else she needs. She, like all the rest, has become a desperate servant.

"Come in, Belinda." I'm still trying to solve the halyard bend knot on the rope nestled in the fur on my lap.

There is nervous laughter. She will try to make sense of her feelings, try to set a tone of sibling comfort and normalcy. She will not be able to hide her fear. She has always bored me.

"I'm sorry to bother you, it's late." The pink froth of her assaulting my senses, the intricacy of that dress and her starched hair offensive.

I pull a hunk of mink up close to my neck. The rope sits limply. "Sit down, sister," I say.

There is the grimace she tries to hide. I know she distrusts our birth connection. I imagine, in her soft, ridiculous little mind, she thinks we are somehow of different seeds. I am so tired of seeing her weep. I will be glad to be rid of her, to ship her off with the Schullers to Germany for a while. She does not sit, as there is nothing comfortable to sit on and every space is covered. Even the hard-carved pew is cluttered with brass trinkets and a vase of unknown dynasty.

She is looking at me at first with curiosity as I toy with the rope. "It's about the wedding…"

"I told you, give our lawyer the bills. Why must you bother me?" I see dawning recognition and a drifting anxiety in her wide eyes.

"Dolores wants to throw the wedding breakfast. I thought I should ask you."

I have conquered the halyard and snap it in the air. "Yes, fine, get it done. What else? I have to dress to go out."

She has lifted a bone white hand to her piqued little mouth and is moving back toward the bleakness of the hallway. "Belasco…"

This particular look of horror has always tickled me. I am anxious to go, to find the dregs of the river, that black creature that supplies me with my vice. I am hungry tonight.

"What is that thing" she says pointing at the long rope. "It can't be."

"What do you think it is, sister?" I say.

"Please, no."

I smile and stifle my laughter. "We must never forget, Belinda. Madness runs in our family. We must acutely remember father's falling, his cowardice. It is who we are. I keep his death noose as a constant reminder. None of we Snopes are safe, my dear, not even you."

She flees before I finish my sentence, the stifled gasp, the rush of slippered feet, the hall door opening and slamming shut. I set the long, gnarled rope aside and prepare for the night.

# FIVE

*A dinner party. A dream. The Garden. Edna arrives.*

*Dolores Brattridge*

ACROSS MY DESK lay a trail of conspicuous names, finely etched on soft white place cards. They demand my attention. Yet through the open doorway is the garden path, the arched entryway of lilac and forsythia, crepe myrtles and violets.

I am vexed by the dull Judge Sterns, a widower who must be seated next to Edna. My dear Edna, will she behave? There will be sixteen for dinner tonight. The cards are pale against my carved mahogany Chippendale secretary, (a gift from Charles' mother who insists that a lady's desk must never be cluttered and seldom be used). I lay my hand across the names, the men and women, flat and uninviting, while just beyond the doorway the garden air is rich, perfumed. Is there time for a walk? Might I sneak a few drops of laudanum into my morning coffee? Dare I, despite the fact that

I have not yet placed the guest of honor, the much-celebrated architect of the Landsworth building, Mr. Clement Cartwright. They say he is extreme, peculiar, and short-tempered. They say he is a genius. I must at least determine his place at the table.

My coffee has gone cold and the wind carries an intoxicating scent of Juniper. I lift my cup. There is a pale blue vein in my hand, like a snaking vine over a landscape otherwise milky. It is a good hand, not as soft now at thirty-five as it was at twenty, wider I think (too large, my mother always said, forever wishing I was petite not stately). That younger hand has been done, molded and confined to a spot on a table near the window. Charles had that hand set in plaster during our engagement *If only he had all of me set in plaster*, I think.

I often wake with terrible thoughts. I have begun to feel obsolete and ugly. I am terrified of madness, of being locked away for incurable melancholy like Beatrice Moore. I look again at my hand. There is something about that threatening blue vein and the ink well with its deep blues, and there, past my desk, through the wide-open doors, the hot blue hydrangea beckoning under a brilliant summer sky. My garden is my escape. They will not cast me in plaster. I will get my hands dirty with earth.

The seating plan is at sea. The Doctor and Mrs. Dandridge shall be at one end of the table. He will go on at length about the violence of the river and she will speak of her family back East, that society. They will mix with the ancient Duchess Brandonshire of Romania, who is startled by very little and deaf in one ear. And what to do with the dreadful, but impossibly rich, Mr. Belasco Snopes and his lovely sister Belinda? I will separate the two of course. She must be near her fiancé, the German beer merchant Heinrich Schuller. And there is the newspaper man, Clarence Dartmouth from New York City. I imagine him to be rough with probing eyes, but Charles insisted. He is writing about our guest of honor, nothing could be done. He had to be invited.

I believe I could make progress on the table, if only I weren't nagged by my garden and also a scant petal of last night's dream, the dream that disturbed me, woke me earlier than usual to come and contemplate tonight's dinner party, then turn away so easily, fussing at that vein, that ink, these names and now ultimately this sky. If only my Charles had told me something about the architect. I will secretly blame him for my mood.

The sun is moving across the lawn. A wind scatters the place cards. Belinda Snopes has fallen to the floor and I let her lie. I will walk in the garden, before the sun is too strong. I dressed for breakfast but kept on my silk slippers. I get up and go to the door. At the threshold, the tiny slope where the doorway meets the lawn, I linger, and for a moment recall the blue of last night's dream. It was the Mediterranean, the most magnificent sea, unblemished by ships, untouched and calm. I was drifting into the water under a bold moon in the dream and there was a beautiful boy. Now, at the doorway, my slippered foot as if on a high wire platform, I hesitate. There is a rustling in the rows of hydrangea and I can see into the pathway which forms a perfect arch of colors distilled in blooms there - pink, scarlet, violet and blood red.

I am still in shadow, not yet into that brilliant morning sun and I feel absolutely reckless, luxuriating in this lost spot, this hesitation between things, this lack of decisiveness or grace. I want to sink my hands in earth up to the elbows. I want to hide the place cards under a bush. I realize who it was I saw ahead of myself in the water, in my dream, I see him, and then I hear Edna.

"I evaded Mrs. Claire and came straight in. That woman is so sour. I don't know why you keep her."

Her voice is strong, dark and masculine, threatening if you did not know her, did not adore her like a sister as I do. Again, she has saved me,

Edna, at my side, taking my hand and pulling me out in to the garden, across the wet grass, my slippers soaked, the lawn terrible, as we move into the day.

"Everyone is talking about Mr. Cartwright. *The Post Dispatch* has done a piece about him and there's the reporter from New York. His great success in Chicago and now St. Louis. And you the first one to throw a dinner party in his honor. You are a sly fox, Dolores. I will tell that to anyone who asks."

"I have been half asleep. You rescued me," I say.

"You need no rescuing dear, don't fuss with me today, I have news that will burn your ears. Your hand is so cold. What were you doing there in the doorway? You did look half-asleep?" she says.

Of anyone, Edna knows my secrets.

"I want you to put me next to Mr. Cartwright at dinner. I saw the seating cards on your desk so I know nothing is set. And please keep me away from that dreadful Eliza Dandridge she is so overly perfumed and such a bore. I can't hear another word about her stunning New York family. You are positively limp. Are you ill?"

She stops us now, just near the arched entry into the garden's center, and turns me, gripping my shoulders. We are the same age, but Edna has always treated me as if she were the older, the wiser which of course she is.

"You're not taking laudanum during the day again are you?" There is such gentleness in her tone. I am overwhelmed but do not want a scene, so I lie.

"No."

We enter the path, surrounded by the vines, the bursts of color. Edna is smaller than I (as most women are) and a lovely, but somewhat exaggerated woman. Everything about her is a bit too much, the rings on her hands, the arch of her nose, the design of her hair. Yet she carries it off, claiming that rubies and mink can cure any ill. She has been a widow (and a Countess with

Italian connections, her husband having died in a fall from a horse after a year of marriage) for nearly a decade. To everyone's surprise she chose not to marry again. She is petite, but commands attention with that dark voice and what some call willfulness. She has never been considered anything but sought after in St. Louis society.

"The things they say about our Mr. Cartwright."

"Don't fill my head with innuendo, Edna, I will not have it."

She laughs and leans into me as we continue. We have entered a private place, and I am free with my words. I can say things I would never repeat outside of this sanctuary. The garden path grows dense, bordered by arching shrubs which climb and meet above our heads, swarming with vine, color and scent. There is a small bench halfway through, a spot where Edna and I have shared dreams for years. We sit in shade, so close that I can no longer discern the aroma of the flowers from Edna's delicate perfume.

"Mr. Cartwright created a mild scandal at the Chicago World's Fair with his golden doorway design. And his Schiller Opera House they say is magnificent, though not everyone supported his coming to our fair city. I believe there was quite a fuss, mostly by Belasco Snopes, though Landsworth being who he is with the Brewers Association snuffed that. And now Cartwright and his partner plan to open an office in St. Louis. I imagine the Snopes' are at wits' end. But one has to pity that family after the tragedy. How could a man with all that money hang himself? At least Belinda has a chance. Anyway, Cartwright is said to be very eccentric."

Edna says things others will not. She is the only woman who can quite often leave me speechless.

"That's enough. I haven't even met the man."

"Well once you do you won't forget him. He is as attractive and as sturdy as the buildings he designs. He was a boxer in his youth and is broad shouldered with the red hair of the Irish."

"That was all in the article?" She laughs and lifts her feet into the air, pointing her toes like a child knowing she has already led me astray. I feel unusual and cannot release an imagined portrait of my guest of honor. I am suddenly, unexpectedly filled with a dark anticipation, as if the summer air were cursed with something wicked, some invisible, intoxicating potion.

"I'm going to tell him about Daisy Sloan's salon. I want him to know our city is not deadly. We have sharp edges," Edna says.

I shudder at the mention of the widow Sloan. She is not the type of woman spoken of in polite conversation. Edna is at times too bold. She takes my hand and squeezes it.

"Will you tell me what is the matter? You can never hide anything from me dear," Edna says.

The warmth of her hand in mine has taken me back to my morning malaise, a sensation of unknowing and sudden wonder that is equally enticing and repulsive. She has drawn close to something I have not yet deciphered within myself. I turn to her, flushed, and then see past her. Mrs. Claire waits at the arched entryway. She is a large dominant woman, a no-nonsense organizer of my household. A savior. We are clearly behind schedule.

"I see that beast. She watches us like a scolding school master. She has always repulsed me," says Edna.

"Where is my mind today? I have so much to do. You need to release me from your spell."

Edna lets go of my hand, stands up, and is moving toward the ominous Mrs. Claire. I wonder if I have wounded her with my tart language. I hurry to her, press my hand into hers, and walk with her toward the house, knowing already that my fears, as always, are unfounded.

# SIX

*A job. Fear in the kitchen. The knife. Escaping with the wine.*

*Calhoun McBride*

HOLDING A STUB between my finger and thumb, stealing a drag in the heat, and thinking how that river's got bits of gold mixed in the mud stink. Night is still and solid black. It's a darkness that seems too heavy.

I'm just outside the kitchen of the biggest house I ever seen up close, here on Vandeventer Place, having a smoke with an Irish kid who got hired for the Brattridge party last minute just like me. He's telling me he made two bucks on poker the night before and I'm ready to find out more when the fat lady cook hollers.

"Ain't paid to sit and jabber. Get in here, boys," she says.

Starting off my big moneymaking scheme by owing that voodoo priestess Bessie for this black and white too damn tight fancy suit just so I could work at this party makes no damn sense. Not a lick. I ain't no servant.

But that Bessie can be pretty convincing. "I got more planned for you. Keep your eyes open at that party. You might be surprised."

*Catch a train. Get on now.*

The kitchen of this grand and golden house is hot. They keep the kitchen side door swung open to the night wind which brings on a sweet scent, something female and wild, blowing from a big garden of flowers out back of the house. I scrubbed hard with lye soap but I still stink of the river.

The kitchen smells better and shines of polished copper. Never seen so much food in one spot. Piles of fish, goose, cheeses, ripe fruits and cakes all orange and red and shimmering, sweet stuff and warm bread that could make a man weep. Never seen so many people working so hard all for one group of fancies.

There's a big mean woman in white, standing hard and steady at a swinging white door that leads to the dining room and I figure she's the captain of this thing. The cook who yelled at me is talking to her and looking hard at me and pointing. I'm still hanging close to the kitchen door, wondering if they might toss me out on my ass any minute.

A fella with tails flies by too fast with a plate of silver and there's a clatter and crash as it all spills. One thin silver knife lands at my foot and without thinking, while he stoops and sweats and hurries to get himself back together, I stick that knife inside my pants and don't even look to see if anybody noticed. That shiny bit might bring me more money than this whole night's work and I gotta start to think smart.

The silver is cold on my inner thigh, held in my drawers on account of the pants Bessie got me are so damn tight. Thinking she might a done that on purpose, dirty old gal. Looking around at this scene—people moving smooth like they was skating on ice, this one chopping, that once scaling, and a girl stirring something in a pot over and over—I know this ain't the right place for me. I'm sweating sure in my gut that this is a rotten idea. I start edging out of the kitchen side door just as two big blokes come in carrying a crate.

"Move out of the way!" A bald man knocks me hard, and I stumble and the knife hidden in my pants cuts into my thigh, and I yelp like a mutt and feel the blood. That mighty lady cook turns to look.

I step outside as they heave the case into the kitchen, blood starting to leak through my pants. I yank the stolen knife out, cussing under my breath. There's a wood box of wine outside, the top open and something tells me to get, to run before they see what I stole and throw me in jail. I'm shaking, thinking what to do, when I hear the hard cry of a night bird like some harking of death and I get that chill I've known in dreams since a boy on the Orphan Train and I snatch a bottle of that port and get away, moving back toward the garden, thinking there's a way out.

Rounding the corner of the house, I meet a wild tangle of color. The back garden is wide and stretches along a narrow path toward an archway that looks like something from church. The garden is lit by the moon and there's a double door from the back of the house spilling out some electric light. I hear the sound of men's voices. I steal past the shrubs and thorny bushes to the archway, back to where it's darker still. I figure there's a wall to hop over.

I'm shaking thinking what a damn fool I am, running like some scared rabbit. At the same time, I'm thinking deep down, *yeah it was good you got out of there.* Frank's right. Scram outta town, catch a train. Hock this bit of silver and go as far as my money will take me. Under these sweet-smelling branches, this thick darkness, I'm feeling dizzy but thinking I finally got it figured out. I'll run off tonight. I'm sick of back-breaking brewery work or back-alley fucking.

There's a bench part way through. Seems as good a place as any to have a nip, clear my head. It's far enough into this path that if anybody figures out I left and comes looking I can run fast out the other end. Though they ain't paid me (except for the bit of silver) so they ain't likely to notice so much. Uncorking the wine takes its time, but I yank a branch, shove it in and make due, leaving some of the cork floating in the redness. Tastes strong. I shut my eyes and set to dreaming, ruminating on the pull of the West, the hope and gold out there. Thinking how a man might steal on a freight train under a hard night moon.

# SEVEN

*A grand dinner. The problem of Snopes.*

*Clement Cartwright*

SIXTEEN SIT FOR dinner. A senator, a judge, a debutante wearing jewels the color of honey, the doddering Romanian Duchess Brandonshire with her ear horn, a newspaper man from New York. Others whose names and titles have faded by the fish course.

I'm a surly guest of honor, silent and brooding, a hapless oaf amongst the gaiety, the polished silver, crystal, mahogany and china. I'd rather be alone with a mutton chop and a whiskey. I need to work up designs for the St. Nicholas Hotel, our firm's next big St. Louis project after the Landsworth. It will rival the Planter's House Hotel here in St. Louis, which is where I am staying. And then there's the reporter across the table who tips his bony head forehead straining to hear my every word. He's been hounding me for an interview. I don't trust him.

My hostess, Mrs. Dolores Brattridge is seated to my right. She turns her face to mine, her eyes steady and imploring, determined to draw me out. For a moment I see the woman sculpted, a stony Venus with strength and mystery in her full face and figure, that crimson pile of hair, the long trail of her arm to pale wrists and strong looking hands. She is not a delicate woman. Stately, graceful and refined like the dining room itself which is all flaming lamps, ancient finery, and magnificent vases overwhelmed with hydrangea, black dahlia, and juniper sprigs.

A footman approaches. Fowl is laid on my plate, covering the plume of a peacock painted on Bentley china. To avoid my hostess' eyes, I grab my wine glass then turn to the large wall across from the dining table with its impressive damask tapestry.

"She is a lioness," Mrs. Brattridge says looking to the damask. "It's thirteenth century Italian."

What I had taken for decorative forest green flourishes on tan is taking shape as a creature with almond-shaped eyes leaping across the tapestry.

"It looks to have hooves," I say. "And to have been cut in half. So, it's a lion?"

My hostess smiles again. She is at the south head of the table, her husband Charles at the opposite end. Gentlemen's voices rise from the north. Mrs. Brattridge leans very close. She brings a calming scent of lavender but I sense a trace of desperation in her voice.

"It is the feminine of the species," she says. "The image is based on an African folk tale, where the creature is said to inhabit the soul of one of the women of the village who had been left by her husband to...to..."

She shuts her eyes and momentarily lilts sideways in her chair. Her face is pale. "I'm sorry, it's the wine," she says.

There is a ruckus from the table's north end. She shifts her eyes to

Belasco Snopes. He is speaking loudly and at length about his family brewery and its upcoming merger with Schuller, the German brewing giant. Snopes is an odd mix of the elegant and the grotesque. He is a young man, just shy of thirty, though his shoulders slope and he hunches in a way that indicates the weight of age. His slickly polished hair, a deep black that conjures eel ink, offers a sharp contrast to his unblemished milky white face which, on a young woman would be considered attractive, but on a man is sickly. He wears a bruise-hued orchid in his buttonhole.

I bristle at the sight of him not only because I consider him a bully, a bore, and a reckless user of cocaine (for supposed ailments), but because he dredges up unpleasant memories of the years my father worked the night shift at Snopes brewery.

"We Snopes were the first ones with the sense to establish a real shipping strategy," Snopes says speaking at a rapid clip. "We Snopes started our own railroad which connects all of our plant's main buildings to the shipping yards near the Mississippi. A stroke of genius if I don't say so myself. And by year's end we Snopes will be shipping beer as far as South America."

He notices me watching him and those black eyes fasten on mine like a vice. I know he despises me.

"How are you finding St. Louis?" Snopes says, moving his hands in a strange circular motion in front of his bony face as if he were casting a spell. "How does it compare to your precious Chicago?"

Ignoring Snopes, the ancient Duchess Brandonshire to my left turns to me and in a very loud voice proclaims: "What inspires a man to become an architect and design something as grand as the Landsworth building, Mr. Cartwright?"

The old woman's voice commands attention. The room has gone dead still.

"It's a fine pursuit," I say.

Snopes snorts. "By which you mean it has financial benefits."

Laughter comes from the portly senator Dew who begins talking about an Arabian horse as the help bring in another course. His story is long and rambling, which allows me time to enjoy the memory of my mother constructing wedding cakes, the real reason I began to imagine and design buildings.

In the memory, I am a phantom. Powdered and pale, my image in the mirror ghostly.

The mirror itself, askew with a hair line fracture down its center, was hung oddly out of place on the wall next to the pantry. It reflected the big oak table where my mother built her wedding cakes and it reflected me, next to her, just tall enough to hover, my hands, cheeks, eyebrows dusted with flour, my fingertips wet with traces of buttercream frosting.

She never shooed me away, instead she would ask my advice as she balanced layers.

"'Even?" she'd say in the heavy Irish brogue I loved but never could mimic.

The harsh clipped German commands from my father, a hard-working and kind, but excessively orderly man, fit my tongue. "Pick it up," he'd say. Or "Tie that lace."

He worked long days, several jobs including carpentry work, shoveling coal on a river boat and those dreadful nightshifts at Snopes Brewery. I believe his economy of speech was a way to preserve energy.

My mother, on the other hand, chattered, sang, told folk tales and even whispered secrets to me when we were alone late in the night, putting together a cake that would be the highlight of a German neighbor's wedding celebration. Building those delicate towers, balancing circle on circle, that was my first love for creation even before I began to wander the streets studying every bit of stone and brick I could find. It was on those streets, too, that I learned to use my fists to make a point, to box for sport and eventual pay, and learned to drink.

As we move to the next course, Senator Dew addresses me. "Come on Cartwright tell us about that Chicago Auditorium you designed. Five hundred seats and seven floors! I read President Harrison himself was at the dedication."

"Yes, I'd say he came as much to hear Mme. Adelina Patti sing as much as see the hall."

"Bah. Humility has no place here. You are the guest of honor and that new building of yours the Landsworth is quite a doozy! The nation's first skyscraper and we've got it."

"It's not the first skyscraper, is it Cartwright?" Snopes says. "That would be the Tacoma building. Yours is clearly second-in-line."

"Whatever it is it's a doozy," Dew says. "And the next one, the St. Nicholas, tell us about that! I hear it will rival the Planter House Hotel on Chestnut Street."

I was not aware the news about our next project had been made public. My eyes stay on Snopes. He has the look of a suddenly cornered beast. His lips curl to a sneer. "They didn't mention that in the article in the *Dispatch*. They didn't mention much of value at all really," he says.

Mrs. Brattridge begins to speak but is cut off by Snopes.

"The article has so little about your early life in St. Louis, the years you lived in the tenement in Soulard, the fact that your father worked like a slave at my brewery," Snopes says. "Are you ashamed of your past?"

I clutch my glass but keep my face still. "No, my family history is not nearly as tragic or as colorful as yours Snopes."

Snopes' scrawny chest puffs and he stands. "My family own large swaths of this town, we have for over a hundred years. We Snopes are the beating heart of St. Louis."

"St. Louis is a magnificent city," I say. "I'm glad to be back."

Mrs. Brattridge stands and raises her glass. "Shall we have a toast to our guest of honor?"

Snopes will not be quieted. "Isn't it ironic that they knew one another, our fathers," he says. "Well maybe my phrasing is off. I don't believe my father spoke much to the line workers. But then your old Papa did not last long before he was fired. I believe he was caught stealing."

"That's a lie." My heart rushing, my arms tensing. "You watch yourself, Snopes." As my blood so suddenly boils, in a moment, I am sixteen on the riverfront, fists raised, defending my family name, my Irish heritage, and my manhood.

But I am not moving at all, not lifting my fists to make contact with his porcelain face, because Mrs. Brattridge has clutched my arm.

"Please, gentlemen," she says.

I turn and notice that she has gone very pale, her mouth agape. Then with a mild whimper, as Snopes begins to laugh softly, she collapses to the floor.

# EIGHT

*Women gather. A phantom in the garden. Belinda's wedding.*

*Dolores Brattridge*

I HAVE FOUND solace at a seat by the window. After my inexcusable fainting, Edna took charge, bless her. Charles must be mortified. How can I face him at bedtime?

The women are momentarily lulled by Caroline, our youngest, at the piano. The men went through with their cigars, opinions and port.

Edna has cozied up to Belinda Snopes. The old Duchess Brandonshire is nodding; her fan spread wide in her lap with its stretched depiction of rosy pink summer nocturne crinum lilies. Outside, in the garden heat, there is a mist before our expected storm. The window blurs with frail drops, and with evening the vines take on something forbidden and dark. Before I turn back to the piano, I glimpse what appears to be a figure rushing past in the garden, taking refuge through the arch of foliage. I should be alarmed but I am not. It was likely a trick of the wind, pulling at the too long vines dancing high, a ruse. It has been a tiring evening and I am not quite myself. And now Caroline's dirge. I have always been unduly moved by music. I need to go to Caroline, to gently touch her shoulder and interrupt her sad yet eager performance before it drags the room into an absolute stupor. Even the ancient Duchess is absent-mindedly pulling her fan slowly closed as if dissolving a lost memory.

Before I can stand, Caroline finishes with a flourish and Edna and Belinda come my way. The Duchess snaps open her fan, a move which indicates the start of a long, slow story for the women near her.

"We are here to revive you," Edna says, settling on a settee side by side with Belinda and facing me.

"You will throw the wedding breakfast for our dear Belinda."

"Belasco agreed," Belinda says with a breathless manner.

The two have stirred me with their glittering tones.

"I promise not to faint," I say.

From my vantage point, I can view the garden through the window which is directly behind the settee. Again, I see a figure moving and this time I do not look away. It is Mr. Cartwright. Edna has launched into her plan and I am able to address her and at the same time watch him. He appears as an errant child, separated from his clan. Hiding, I imagine. He is a large bull of a man, broad shouldered, thick, that mane of red hair, yet there is something delicate about the way he moves as if he were afraid to disturb the night air. He pauses, looking around with innocence and wonder. Then he escapes through the archway.

"You both are sisters to me," Belinda says. "You are all I have. Belasco can be so...strange. I'm afraid he's still obsessed over Father's death."

She touches me, this girl, this odd untarnished pearl in a family shadowed with blackness. I have often hoped she would escape (as she will by marrying Heinrich Schuller) though now as it is happening, I feel a secret regret, as if she will flee with a younger part of my self.

Caroline has sat at the piano again, and begins a cheerful tune at the Duchess's urging. I turn once more to the garden but there is no one there, and heavier drops strike the glass, drumbeats stirring me in ways unwanted and unknown.

# NINE

*Escape to the garden.*

*Clement Cartwright*

I AM ASSAULTED with the songs of the night, of cicadas and locusts. There are scents of lemon, wisteria, juniper and rose. The garden is wild, lush. It calms my temper. I cannot afford to wrangle with Snopes until the St. Nicholas deal is settled, so I left the gentlemen as they cut their cigars.

I step into the garden through a dying mist to get a good look at the moon. It is bold and white, though clouds in the distance race to devour it. I recall sweltering summer nights like this, swimming in the river under a full moon, my father watching from the shore. He would not join me, and as my toes hit the murky water he would shout, "Mind the current."

There were nights I would float on my back, spying a river boat in the distance. Bright, glittering things, the noise of music and voices beginning low, then building until I could discern stray phrases or individual laughter.

I once swam close enough so that waves gushed down my throat from the wake of the stern and powerful paddle wheel. I did not tell my father when I swam back to shore. I wonder if there were things he never told me. Did he truly get fired from Snopes' Brewery?

The garden is alluring. Mr. Charles Brattridge seems ordinary, another gray skinned investor, but this garden was not hatched from the mind of a dullard. It is the creation of his wife. I would like to get to know her.

I move further into the garden, wander toward an archway. It is a place to enter, to hide, to waste time until it is acceptable for the guest of honor to leave. I have a sudden urge to get away from this party, to run down to the river and wash off the vile stink of Belasco Snopes.

I approach the trellised archway, leading further into this little oasis. The wild veiny leaves rope up and over forming a caved entry, dangling fingerling vines, deeply purple. Stepping into the jaws of blackish green, the air rain-scented, I am struck with a wave of loneliness. I have not wandered the dark shores for so long. There is a rumble of thunder, a cry of a riverboat whistle in the distance. I turn back anxious to take my leave, and get down to the river, that rough place of my youth.

# TEN

*The river runs red. The bone necklace. A realization.*

*Calhoun McBride*

NEARING THE RIVER, I fall hard on the railroad tracks at the pitch of the hill and throw up all that red wine. Rain's coming down hard, cobblestones spit shined and night-slick. My insides rush like a stream down to the Mississippi and I think now my guts are in that river, now I'm part of that bigger thing. Hole in my pants, cut on my thighs leaking, that mixing with my gut-wine, all that flowing down the hill. The river's running red, like God opened a vein to bleed his wrath.

I lay my cheek on the track metal, cool in damned heat, thinking I don't care two hoots if a cargo train comes on by and squashes me to shit, cuts me into a thousand pieces, hunks of me flying off to a river grave. Maybe I should leave tonight. Maybe I'm a damn fool.

I get up off of the railroad tracks and go down to the river's edge, splash my face, trying to unravel the crazy night. I take off my shirt, stand and stretch. With the sudden rain coming down so hard, over my face and chest, it's like swimming. I squint, looking through a million drops, deciphering a blur of black sky and rain and river.

"I made a dirty mess of this!"

My voice is puny against the storm, the rushing Mississippi. I move away from the river's edge and go sit down and think. I got away from the party and nobody seemed to notice. At least I got one piece of silver. I need to talk to that voodoo sorceress Bessie. What did she have in mind sending me to that job? I ain't never been inside a house like that and don't know nothing about service. She'll cut me a new asshole and call me yellow for running. Still, I need to talk to the old witch. She was sure right about a storm coming. This one came on fast.

"Keep your eyes wide open and your head clear," she'd said.

We was in Frank's shack. He was passed out. I was getting dressed in the fancy servant clothes for the party. Bessie was drinking, watching, speaking in that low slur that always gives me the shakes.

"Come here boy," she said.

I skulked over and she put a skinny necklace with a shred of bone round my sunburnt neck.

"It's good luck, will guide you. I got a feeling about tonight. The moon's near-full, and that means lovers are lucky. But you gotta be smart, you hear me?"

I was itchy in that suit and tired of her voodoo predictions and rattling.

"Things ain't always like they seem, might be some magic," she said, all sick with mystery, sipping at her cooch wine.

The rain lets up and stops. I touch the bone necklace, then see a fella coming down the hill. A swell looking for trouble I'm guessing. He's tall, suited, a redhead. Handsome. He's stumbling over the cobblestones down to the river's edge. He don't see me. I'm sitting near the Eads Bridge in shadow. It's a darker patch of the levee.

Near the water, he sits his ass down and starts yanking at his shoes until he's wrangled them off. He lays back, staring at his stocking feet then he takes a gander up at the dark sky. Hard rain will be coming down steady and warm.

A long, sad rumbling from above. He tilts his head up, then stands, looks out at the river. Then he goes at his shirt, getting it off, tossing it, then the pants. He's moving pretty quick, steady, like the threat of the storm and the call of the river got to him. He's down to his drawers then he shucks them, too, and hollers, running out to the water. There's a stony hardness to his body, the tough muscle of a boxer but with a thick sturdiness I'd like to get ahold of. He don't look like a city fella undressed. I shudder, my mind going fast with want, and I don't care. I get up and head after him in that water for a swim.

At the shore, the loose brown waves are tipping steady. He's already in, hollering. Just as I step in I can see, in that curling water, his head bobbing. He's treading and he sees me at the shore, watching him, and I think maybe he's waiting for me. The water slops at my feet and I stay like that, at the lip of it, not moving. He waves and I get naked, feeling him watching me. I think how tonight the river looks copper, not brown, like the clouds tore open and bled down into the mud, put some blood-life in that old Mississippi. Then I feel another raindrop.

"Hey," I holler.

I can't see him. He swum out further. I dive in and move steady, toward where I'd last seen him. Rain's starting. A rip of lighting and the sky goes white and I hear three hard thunder rolls and then hear him shout. I swim harder and near run into him in the dark waves.

"Magnificent," he says, his head bobbing up and down.

We're both slurping water. A wind strikes up and I see coming round the bend the Gypsy Queen riverboat. She's gonna toss a good wake at us.

"Come on! Let's get back to shore. Big wake."

The boat's not in our path but close enough to send a bad roll of waves. It's getting closer. I point my arm toward shore and start swimming that way but turning back, I see he's not moving. The Gypsy Queen is coming closer and there go the waves. He pitches up and down and then goes under. I swim over fast, and he's surfaced again shouting and I grab him and pull him to me, hoisting him up so we ride them waves together, his wet eyes on mine, and that's when I know we're both after the same thing, us thrashing close in that mean water, him gripping at me while the boat passes, then me pulling him closer. In the wild wave, I push my face close to his, lips on his cheek, then see his wide searching eyes surprised and I taste the wet hair and us two slurping river water, barely staying up, and all the sudden he somehow gets his lips on me, too, and I know what's going on and it ain't no dream. I shudder like heaven cracked open.

The boat passes and he breaks away and swims to shore and I follow. He crawls out, grabbing his clothes. I get out and get mine, then walk over to my hidden sleeping place under the shadow of the big Eads Bridge. He follows. The shore's still empty and the rain's coming on a little harder. No more thunder, just a slow steady rain, and I wonder how long 'til the river rises higher. How long 'til she bursts with flood.

We hunch there under the bridge, against its cool stone back. He's breathing easier. He pulls a silver flask from his coat pocket sips and passes. The rain puts out a softer sound now, like a creek rushing. He struggles to get up on both knees to face me, falling once, then tries again.

"You gonna tear up your knees," I say.

He's facing me, all that wild hair damp and scattered. The river streaked his cheeks with its muddy stain. He's staring hard at me and I lean into him. He pulls me close and sets in on kissing and chewing my lip, his hands gripping my head harder and harder, and I grab his head and try to pull him into me, though he can't likely get no closer.

We're fastened to one another and I'm falling into his scent. I grip a bunch of hair and we lay back and he's on top of me and he's heavier than I imagine. I try to get a quick look down the shore but the rain's coming even worse now, which is good since ain't nobody like to be out. There's nothing lurking through the haze.

I need more of him and I'm not caring two shakes if he pays me or not. He's not like the others. I'm sinking into this thing we done started, not even sure what this means to a man like him, but knowing what it means to me, and there's that freckled naked chest. I go at that with my tongue and mouth and he's getting mangier, cocky now, tough, and he whispers something I can't make out and we set into more kissing, then we manage to roll down closer to shore, the rain spraying and the shore water lapping. I can taste his neck and feel his soft hands and we start making a ruckus like mad beasts, but I don't care. I flip on my belly and a muddy wave slaps us and he gets on me and I know somehow this is crazy different, like something I never done before. There ain't nothing to stop us, and I think, don't ever leave, never leave me, and there's only his hand in my hair and the feeling of angels in the rain, whispering to me, taunting me, telling me to live.

# ELEVEN

*A dramatic announcement. Charles and the Orient.*

*Dolores Brattridge*

CHARLES INSISTS ON silencing the hot night, shutting the bedroom window though I wish he would not. I am unraveling after the party, a success he says. Off handedly, as he fusses at a tangled ivory button on his shirt sleeve, he announces we will have a telephone, and that he will be going to the Orient for two months this summer. I am more startled by the concept of the telephone, its disruption, though I turn from my dressing table. I am not sure how to address him.

Thankfully, he begins. "There is a golden bit of opportunity, and I cannot pass this up. Damn this thing. Who will sort things like this out for me over there? That will be something else."

I rise and go to him, firmly grasping the reckless shirt button, yanking it like a tooth, quieting him. He takes my hand.

"I did not want to tell you until after the party. I know how important these things are for you. But there's no avoiding it. And it would be impossible for you to join me. It's barbaric to even mention that."

He releases my hand and I smile, noticing the tufts of gray at his temple, the still stirring blue of his eyes, that ruddy skin. He is a tall, striking man. Returning to my table, I deposit the button and begin my toilette. I want to inquire about the telephone and whether I will have access to our accounts or if I will have to go to our estate lawyer Mr. Ransdale. I hope he allows me some freedom. Ransdale is elderly, stingy, and smells of licorice and cigar smoke. But those are not the right things to say at the moment.

"It will be difficult to get along without you, Charles. Is it safe over there? I've heard stories. "

He has settled in a side chair and is watching me.

"Don't go reading "Confessions of the Orient". That's all rubbish. It is no place for a woman, of course, but I will make due. God knows St. Louis in August is ghastly. I am not sure which of us may be more miserable."

I turn. He is very still. I want to go to him, to ruffle his hair, to reach for his hand. He has always been kind to me.

"What will you do with yourself?" he says sleepily.

I am at my vanity table finishing my hair, and there behind me in the mirror is some translucent shadow which I imagine as Edna. She has coaxed me so many times to join her, to wander to a daring salon, an opera, to steal away unaccompanied and it has become our secret girlish chatter, our phantom fantasies. What will she suggest in Charles' absence?

"Could we open the window for just a few moments, Charles, it's so warm," I say.

He laughs, then goes to the window, opens it and stays there, gazing out at my garden. "He's an odd one, the architect Cartwright. Don't you think? He's not easy to talk to."

"He seems very determined," I say. "He's accomplished so much. It must keep his mind occupied."

Charles walks over to me to touch my shoulder. "You are so kind."

He releases me and leaves the room and I stop with the brush, recalling our guest of honor Mr. Cartwright and the few moments we shared. He had been shy, uncomfortable and clearly brutalized by the horrendous Mr. Snopes. His eyes revealed both a tremendous sadness and vibrancy. I wished I had taken the time to find out what caused that grief. After dinner, sitting with the women, I had seen him through the window, as he pierced the garden archway, into my private place, there with the juniper. Perhaps there will be time this summer to learn more about our ubiquitous neighbor, perhaps that will be part of my summer dreaming as my Charles sails away from me.

I stare at my hair brush with its ivory handle, but I do not pick it up.

# TWELVE

*Jenny Claire. A hidden shack. A man's vice.*

*Belasco Snopes*

SHE WILL BE waiting blind-folded, on dark knee naked, that Jenny Claire. We meet in the thatched wooden sanctuary I keep at river's edge. It's a hot, black midnight and I'm ravenous. It's been too long since I've lay on the dirt floor of my secret river hut, felt earth on my naked back, dug my toes in things dank and untouchable, smelled the root of women like Jenny. The throwaways, the vile ones.

It will be our last meeting, though pretty Jenny will want more now that I've seduced her with the gentle shots of cocaine and the laudanum. She asked for it last time. What would she do for it tonight? One more visit little Jenny, then off with you. I'll tell the whore monger Bessie to find me a new plaything. I've nearly tired of sweet Jenny.

I have always had my secret places, since a boy. My tunnels, my caves, my hiding spots in woods deep or gardens overgrown. Scented, deadly things all. This one was hatched from the womb of that Voodoo Negress Bessie one summer night last year not long after daddy's cowardly hanging. I was slumming on the river, drunk but alert, craving the underbelly of our city, sick of the dinner parties and recitals. I was still seething over Daddy's vile escape.

I'd found Bessie in the corner of a dank saloon dressed in feathers and gold like a delirious gypsy. I told her I wanted to touch things disgusting that night. She said that every man needs a woman like Bessie. I saw the truth in that. She's smart enough to stay quiet, greedy to the core, with nimble hands on the edge of things both diabolical and civilized in this city. She soon learned what I wanted and found me my hideaway, my play pen, my toys.

The hut sits in a place of shadowy squalor, just up the hill from the river on torn cobblestones, not far from the rail tracks. Bessie owned it, a gift from a long-ago river boat suitor she said, and she sold it to me, followed my instructions of getting it painted tar black, blotting the windows, stocking it with the things I wanted, the potions and instruments. Bessie asks no questions. Bessie earns her way.

The river is still. I stop, lift my pant leg, and inject myself with cocaine. Tonight, I am drawn to the solid darkness out there, that dank water. I am feeling the first tingling rush and am anxious to get to Jenny, to begin. There is no time to test myself, to dip my ankle, to see if the water hisses with rebuke. Perhaps I can bring her back, dip her in like a tea bag, and hold her there until she squirms. Will we even get that far tonight?

The hut is a blot on the nightscape, unnoticeable, black and plain. I push the thick front door and enter. There she kneels, as I told her. She is bone thin, busty, a mane of hair henna dyed and ratted high in a feeble attempt at fashion. I see her head dart, her tongue loll. She is hungry for the drug. Behind her is the bar. I move there gently, quietly, and prepare a laudanum tonic. I touch her hair, pull her head back, and feed her the stuff. She gulps. Then I sit in a high back chair near the whip which had belonged to my great grandfather Jedidiah Snopes. She is breathing quickly, her head swaying side to side. I know she wants it. I am relieved in that gentle place of knowing, of thrusting myself higher on the throne that is Snopes, overseeing and cleansing as Daddy did, finally breathing evenly after so many long hours of horrid mediocrity and the drabs. I slowly let the debris of life dissolve into the river-soaked wood floor: Belinda, Cartwright, the drags, even Daddy hanging like mere bone and flesh, cracking, thrown to the dogs, when we both know he will transcend. He is watching me now.

There is a feeble muttering. She has waited long enough, my Jenny. I rise and begin my magnificence.

# THIRTEEN

*Bessie's place. Vodoo. That necklace.*

*Calhoun McBride*

SOMETHING STEWING UP a stink in a big black pot on the wood stove. I'm thinking it's crawfish swimming in boiling river water. Bessie's stirring slow and steady. I'm sitting at a table made up of trees uprooted from the last big flood. Fat Frank crafted it for her.

"Don't you bleed on my floor you son of a bitch," she says. "Hold that rag tight on that thigh 'til I make up my mind to fix ya."

After the fella at the river (my name's Cartwright he said boldly, come see me at the Planter House hotel) I found Fat Frank and he brought me straight to Bessie's place. Years back, she took hold of this ratty cellar under a saloon that sits right off the riverfront. Frank, who's taking a nap in back, holes up here as much as at his own shack.

Only way to get in Bessie's place is from the outside through a thick wood trapdoor at street level. Stepping down into the black is like sinking into some bad snake-licked nightmare. It's dark and right away you smell tobacco and whiskey and other wild things, spicy and hard like that crawfish she's cooking now.

She's got the place cozied up with junk you might expect in a fortune teller's tent. Wild striped animal pelts, velvet hanging off the walls, crazy bleached skulls and bones of all sorts, and a whole mess of clocks made from brass, glass and wood. I once asked her why she don't sell them fancy clocks and she shook her head said "Boy, time ain't for sale." There's a mess of paintings on the walls too, ugly clown faces and fancy looking fellas wearing big hats, then a fat man in a uniform holding a gun. I never guessed Bessie woulda hang up pictures like that.

"You crazy sonabitch coming round to see Bessie after what you done?" she says. "Made me look like a fool. I go to all the trouble of setting you up for that job then you run off scared like a stinky white rabbit."

I hear springs bounce on the cot in back where Frank's sleeping. Bessie turns fast to look at me, then she laughs, loud and ragged and smacks a spoon on that old black pot. She's wearing a frilly white dress and a bunch of yellowed pearls round her black neck. The air feels oily, and I hold back a notion to sneeze. The rag is soaked red on my thigh.

"What you bring me to drink?" she says.

Frank warned me about that. Never show up at Bessie's without liquor. I set the hooch on the table then whip out a sneeze and she turns to me. I see the white of her eyeballs.

"I ain't a hard woman. I give everybody one chance. Tell me: what made you run? Don't lie or I'll throw this hot soup on your leg."

She's still stirring that pot. Frank's snoring has a nice rhythm. My hands are shaking so I reach for the bottle and take a glass off the table and pour myself a shot.

The spoon stops. A tiny varmint skits across my foot and I want to jump up but stay still and keep my eyes on Bessie.

"You best start talking fore I lose my patience boy!" she says. "I ain't in no mood today."

Frank grumbles a little in his sleep, something about a fight, then rolls over. Bessie sits down across from me at the table. I check the floor but whatever was creeping over my feet done scrammed. I take a deep breath, then set into telling her the story, sticking with the truth, even about the silver knife I snatched and about the fella I met at the river.

I spill it all, hoping that she rips into one of them big belly laughs calling me a fool. Instead, she goes quiet. Then she pulls up a butt from somewhere and flares a match. With a long skinny finger piled with three gold rings she pulls a shred of tobacco off her tongue.

"You wearing the bone?"

I reach under my shirt and pull out the bone necklace she gave me.

She reaches a hand and holds the thing, then shut her eyes and mumbles something. She opens her eyes and stares right into me. "That bones real hot, boy. That bones on fire."

"I been running."

She drags on her flaring butt and smiles. "You so lost," she says in a whisper.

Then she reaches over and grabs my hand, shuts her eyes and sets into humming. I'm wishing Fat Frank would wake up just about now. Bessie gets still.

"You in this thing now, you done brought it on," she says. "Now what you gonna do?"

She's still got my hand and I swear them crawfish are starting to cry a little from the pot.

I'm sweating. "What you mean?"

She leans forward, squeezing my hand hard. "The moon's like that bone on fire tonight. Sent beams on you, picked you out somehow, and giving you a chance," she says. "I never could account for why some get a blessing and others don't. Even fools like you. But it done happened and now you need to decide."

My hand is hurting and my face is wet and hot. "What do I need to decide?"

"You gonna go back and find him, that fella you met, you gonna stare in the face of that moon fire and ask for what you really want, or you gonna turn tail and run," she says.

Finally, she lets go and we sit listening to the wind and Fat Frank's snoring. "Hear that wind? I told you a storm was coming. This ain't no gentle rain. There's something black and terrible coming down. Bessie knows. And it ain't stopping soon."

She goes back to humming, a gentle song in some language I never heard and with her eyes shut she looks sort of peaceful. I'm pretty sure she's crazy, but truth is that bone does feel hot on my chest, and I can't stop thinking one thing. *Get on back, get on back.* Ain't nothing else in my head, no matter how I search. *Get on back and see Cartwright* again soon.

"Now let's get that leg fixed up. Grab some whiskey I think you need a stitch or two on that," Bessie says, going to fetch her medicine kit.

# FOURTEEN

*A visit to Daisy Sloan. The violinist. Fainting again.*

*Dolores Brattridge*

I STRUGGLE WITH what to wear to the salon of divorcee Daisy Sloan. I choose a nondescript Tulip Bell skirt and an ivory shirtwaist along with a veiled hat and gloves, despite the heat. Once in the carriage, I feel undone. Charles is gone barely two weeks, and I am already making reckless choices. I scold Edna, and tell her to turn back, suggesting we reroute our late day outing to the St. Louis Choral Society.

"What would Charles think? I'm already falling in with a theatrical crowd," I say.

"Stop it, you are not a snob, Dolores, though you try to act it," Edna says. "You need a diversion so you don't worry about Charles during his long journey to the Orient. I won't let you fall into a laudanum stupor."

She refuses to reconsider our adventure, distracting me with a vivid story about the supposed affair Daisy Sloan had last winter with a Russian Duke who kept a leopard as a pet.

Upon entering her smallish townhouse, Daisy comes to us directly, speaking in a hushed tone, taking my hand and guiding me to a seat on a fainting couch in the rear of her cramped, striking sitting room. She speaks freely, gently and kindly, complimenting my appearance and thanking me for making the trip. It is not at all what I expected.

Sitting alone on the couch, I choose tea, refusing champagne for fear it will make me dizzy. It is late afternoon and I wonder what Charles is thinking en route to Shanghai. He dismissed my last-minute appeals that he not go (or at least not flee so rapidly with such little notice!) pointing out that His Royal Highness the Duke of Connaught visited Shanghai this year. I read that the Duke had brought his wife, Princess Louise of Hohenzollern, but I did not mention that to Charles.

I watch Edna who is boldly talking to a raffish red-headed poet across the room. I will not stay long. There is something very wicked about all of this. In my sequestered corner, I lift the veil off of my face, a move which feels girlish and reckless. I am not a child, I think. This is harmless. To leave immediately would be fussy and discourteous.

It is a long, narrow, and spare ladies' sitting room with a front alcove space. One wall is lined with deep red-bound books (likely pages left uncut as I cannot imagine Daisy Sloan sharing my interest in literature). There is an oversized embroidered foot stool, an odd tapestry hanging haphazardly as well as several vases of rust colored, exotic blooms. I consider removing my hat, but am struck by what my Charles would say upon entering, finding me hidden in the rear, uncovered. He would not scold me, rather frown, his forehead a canvas of wrinkles, and he would say "It's very warm," which I would understand to mean "we must leave." He would excuse my eccentricity, blaming Edna, and we would go off and dine.

There is music. A light slow melody made with a bowed instrument coming from within the alcove area. Past Edna and the obese red headed poet in tweeds, the music rises in volume. I believe it is a violin. I cannot see the musician but the music disturbs me and I imagine he is dark, like a gypsy. It is not frantic or obscene, but rather sad and too slow. I imagine Charles at sea, crossing the ocean. It is night and the waves would be black to him. The musician lightly taps his foot. The large poet has moved and I can now see that speck of him, his horned shoe. I must leave very soon.

The music moves swiftly, trilling up, and I flush, and I know yes, yes, I must go, that my initial sensations of ease were a ruse. The room grows increasingly hot. "Enough" I say softly to myself, as if to Charles. "I do not belong here, had no business coming." The music escalates with a new forbidding rhythm and it is too reminiscent of imagined music halls I long ago fantasized. I am about to rise when two bold young women rush in from the street. They are moving toward me, smiling, then are sitting and sharing the large oval footstool, their backs to me. I am in slight shadow, wearing nothing vivid, and it seems to me that in their haste they did not notice me, or perhaps saw me as a blended image of the drab wallpaper. It is the type of rudeness I expect at an artist's salon. I am satisfied now that my decision to flee is correct. I realize I would like Charles to rescue me. But he is gone. If only I could get Edna's attention.

The two women are flushed of face and talking rapidly, finishing a long story, both pale in complexion and very pretty. I recognize one as the actress Maude Adams from New York. I read about her performance in the play *Lord Chumley* and wonder if she is in our city as part of the Landsworth building opening. It is quite an event.

The two women are drinking champagne. The violin is moving at a ridiculous pace. I will need to get past these women. I must get up.

"That's what he said," Maude says.

"Impossible," says the other, loudly, slovenly.

"He saw it," says Maude, laughing in short staccato breaths, in time with the awful violin.

I am motioning to Edna.

"They call her Bessie. She's river trash. But she's not a real she at all. She's a man done up, all trussed up like a circus act. And she has a real bust!" says Maude. "And then there's this place…"

Her voice lowers to a whisper. The other girl begins laughing loudly and I rise and move past them toward the door, clutching my hat and I am very, very hot and I see the violinist and it is as if there was a sudden turn in a hallway where hovered a basket of serpents because he is sweaty and dark and I pass Edna and go toward the front door ignoring her calls to me. I fear if I pause to talk to Edna I will be lost and also, that man, that violinist has the blackest hair I have ever seen and black eyes and I am frightened and I say it aloud, I say "Charles," then at the door coming toward me is someone I recognize, the architect Mr. Cartwright and I think *I have been discovered*, and all goes so very hot and white and I am gone.

# FIFTEEN

*A dream. Mr. Cartwright's kindness. Dearest Edna.*

*Dolores Brattridge*

I WAKE THINKING: The river will run red.

There is a large window, no, it is not a window rather a set of French doors and there are no drapes. Struggling to wake I am startled to see through the glass doors locusts hiving in waves across the sky as if held together by a river of rain. I recall a story where the locusts came and the rivers ran with blood. It is extremely hot in this room and there is no air.

"Charles?" I call, trying to sit up.

He is likely near, unruffled, assuring me my fever will pass by the end of August. He told me: "The orient is no place for a woman. You are weak Dolores." I cannot seem to move my hand. I am lying on a settee, near the set of doors and then I realize: "That is my garden."

I sit up. Slowly I piece myself together. I fainted. We were at that vulgar salon, Daisy Sloan. I am still dizzy and now coming toward me is the architect Mr. Cartwright who saved me as I fell. His broad ruddy face is framed with a wild mane of red hair. I remember him as he was the night of our dinner party earlier this month. I recall him escaping through the vines. The room is still but the storm is chaotic. It is raining heavily. There are no locusts, no biblical demands. Edna pushes past Mr. Cartwright, handing me a glass of Sherry.

"Drink this, slowly," she says.

She takes my hand and I see the concern in her eyes. I try to speak but words are heavy.

"I am so..."

Edna stops me, quiets me. Mr. Cartwright lingers behind her. His eyes meet mine and he is familiar. It is as if we had met long ago.

"She is prone to fainting, and I suppose today I am to blame," says Edna, turning to draw Mr. Cartwright into the conversation. "Her husband left the country, and I have been keeping an eye on her. I thought an excursion would do her good but I was mistaken. She has always been delicate."

Edna speaks directly to him as if I were asleep and I do not like it. I must salvage this situation. I must be hostess in my own home. I sit up.

"Thank you, Edna, but I am to blame. I had not eaten. I was foolish." I say. "I am so sorry to have troubled you Mr. Cartwright"

He comes closer. "You saved me from Daisy Sloan."

I find his tone direct. I believe him to be a kind and honest man.

"Please call me, Clement," he says. "I'll let you rest."

I can see, past him, the torrents of rain slashing up my garden. "Wait for the storm to settle," I say.

He smiles. "I have an appointment but I'd like to stop in another time to see how you are if that's all right?"

"That's kind of you," Edna says.

I meet his eyes again. They hide very little.

"Are you sure you can't wait out the storm?" I say.

"I'm meeting Belasco Snopes, not a man to keep waiting."

"How dreadful!" Edna says. "I put up with him only because of his charming sister Belinda."

Mr. Cartwright smiles. "I'm a business man. I don't need to like our investors."

"Is he investing in the Landsworth Building?" Edna says.

"He's interested in our next venture, a hotel we plan to call the St. Nicholas," Cartwright says. "He's prominent in this city, that's clear."

I try to sit up but think better of it. I will not faint twice in one day.

"Thank you again," I say.

"I can see myself out," he says.

He takes his leave and Edna comes to me.

"What is the matter with me," I say softly. "I am going to pieces."

She takes my hand, kisses it, resting near me, as she has so many times, before and during my marriage, through discoveries and disturbances. Her presence, I know, will always be soothing. There is a terrible crash of thunder, but neither of us is bothered.

# SIXTEEN

*The Snopes'caves. Mr. Cartwright. Daddy watches.*

*Belasco Snopes*

WE SNOPES MEN will forever keep these hushed, wet caves that snake under the family brewery deliciously dark. Daddy did, as will my some-day son

The only entry to the caves is by way of a ragged rope ladder that dangles from the factory above like a serpentine tongue. There is a three-foot drop from the ladder's last wrung into the blackness of the caves. Oil lanterns hang and sway dimly from the high rock ceiling, leading maze-like to the Mississippi River five blocks away. The lamps are weak and leave long intricate hollows of darkness in this underground chamber. The walls are jagged and twist sharply, following first a straight line then opening wide like beastly jaws dropping as the path moves toward the riverfront. The caves store hundreds of barrels of beer. Hour after hour, men young and old hoist and haul things on strained back from carved out chilling spots straight to the riverboats.

"A sweet place of bleak shadows between slivers of light. It keeps men off balance," Daddy said.

He struck some of his best deals down here, guiding men through the rocky maze, throwing them ever so slightly off base as he claimed a stake in their business, or convinced them to sell their souls.

He took me to a very private place in the caves when I was seven. An area several hundred feet from the western entrance, roped off and hidden from the workers. There is a carved out hollow in the rock wall, a hard-jagged man-made opening leading deeper into granite, to a second rope ladder that leads up to a manmade platform and a throne unseen, this all created by Daddy to reign over those he did not trust.

"Only allow a Snopes into this private place," he told me the first time he revealed his shadowy throne. "Anyone else that discovers it must be discarded."

On the platform sits his throne, a 16th century Italian Sgabello owned at one time by Pope Alexander VI whose nefarious reign was laced with bribery, murder, simony and incest. The throne is both intricate and harsh. The base consists of a high but narrow bench, this topped with a wooden octagonal box. The throne's back is an elaborately carved piece of mahogany shaped like an inverted V that rises five feet toward the heavens. Gems line the edges of the throne, and menacing nude cherubs drip off the pointed top as if held in suspension before being cast to hell. The throne rises high on the rock platform, giving a view through an opening carved into the rock.

From my hidden perch here on the throne, I watch them toil. Hunched men scurrying rat-like at their tasks, half blind, hoisting barrels, whispering that we are frugal, we Snopes, we dirty outliers not fit to shine their shoes, we Louisiana trash swimming up river some hundred years ago to conquer

St. Louis. They do not know I hear every word, record every movement from my perch.

It is my place of reigning. I can give myself my cocaine injections here unseen. I have my leather kit and my needle. I will use the snaky vein near my ankle; the veins on my arms are too bruised. I have taken to wearing long sleeves in this dreadful heat.

I am careful. I will not let the drug wreck me as it did Daddy, the fool, hanging himself in a crazed fit of despair leaving me a mess of debts and bad deals, forcing me to get in bed with the German beer barrens the Schullers, to rush a wedding, to nearly auction off my sister Belinda (though luckily, she believes it is love and Heinrich is devilishly attractive).

Daddy did not understand how to use cocaine to properly embrace euphoria to achieve greatness. I have read everything Dr. Freud has written about the mind accelerating drug, the wonder of it. I have control over it because we Snopes are of mind's superior (Daddy's lapse withstanding). I prepare the needle and feel the tiny prick. The mild rush. I will not think of Father or his ridiculous failure, I will think of my coming pawn, that fool from Chicago Clement Cartwright who has already stolen so much from me, who is trying to swoop in and take over deals in my city that are not his to have. He will be taught to honor and respect the Snopes' name. He will be made to understand. I am floating here waiting. My invitation was succinct.

"We got off on the wrong note regarding the St. Nicholas Hotel deal. Please come have a tour of my brewery. I have a proposition you are sure to find financially appealing."

I have not been able to gain a full stake in the St. Nicholas Hotel deal, but I will not lie down and let that scum, that river trash whose father all but licked my Daddy's heels rolls over me. I will find his weakness. I will get under his skin. Then I will slip into that deal, I will turn around our family's financial losses and stop the hemorrhaging cash.

My skin is tingling; the coolness of the cave calms me. The scraping of the barrels is a melody. I envision momentarily Cartwright's blood rushing, flowing from a beer spicket, flooding the river red, his bludgeoned body sinking and his filth dissolving. The St. Nicholas deal mine. Feed the river, Daddy said. It gets hungry.

Through the wall I watch the rope ladder.

There he is, emerging from the main factory above, climbing down the ladder rungs into the cave swaying for a moment, then letting go and dropping to the floor. He stops, eyes adjusting, waiting.

Cartwright is alone.

How long will he wait there, how long before the stillness, the darkness, the long dreadful quiet and moist chill will cause him to move, to go back up, or to go further in, to seek what I imagine he is clearly after. I believe he means to ruin me. I believe he knows far more than he says about my secrets, my vices. I believe he has a plot darker and more intricate than mine. He means to conquer St. Louis and ruin the Snopes' strong hold. I know this. He will need to be gutted and hung to dry.

"Mr. Cartwright." My voice, from above, carries gently. I hurry down, glimpsing his dismay, his confusion, and I suppress laughter. I emerge from the black, into the entry way light, into his space, too close, startling him.

"Why are we down here?" he says loudly, stepping back, nearly knocking into the still-swaying ladder behind him. "What are you up to Snopes? Don't you have a proper office where we can meet?"

"This is a very special place. I don't invite everyone down for a tour of the caves," I say.

I am pleased. I touch his shoulder, and he recoils. Then he unexpectedly, too boldly, damn him, he steps ahead of me into the black.

"Wait," I say, following.

"What is it you want to show me?"

"Most men wait for my guidance."

"It's like a tomb."

"Stop," I say.

In the still darkness, he stops. I wonder if he trembles.

"It is much like a crypt, yes. Outside the temperature may reach one hundred degrees but here, down under, it remains cool, the beer we store stays fresh. And the tunnels, they run straight to the docks, to the river boats. Let's walk," I say.

"It's a strange way to talk business," he says. "What's on your mind? You mentioned a financial prospect."

I regain the lead, moving at a clip. We pass the men, the drabs, the stray lanterns. The drabs do not look up. They fear I would carve out their eyes. I am shivering with excitement and would love one more injection. But not yet.

"These caves, this brewery, it is part of this city's history. We are an institution," I begin. "Now that you are building here, you need to know what we stand for, where we have come from."

"I don't follow," Cartwright says. "Why don't you hang more lights?"

He trips, regains. I move more swiftly.

"I'm interested in investing in the St. Nicholas Hotel," I begin. "I know things have moved along, but you would be smart to have a man like myself involved. A respected local man. A Snopes. There are things I can do to help with the city council."

He is struggling to keep up.

"Look, Snopes, we offered you stock in this and you turned us down. The offer we made stands."

"I'm not looking for a small percentage, I want a proprietary stake in the property," I say.

"You know our offer. Nothing has changed. And I've seen enough of this tomb. I thought you had something important to tell me. This has been a waste of my time."

I stop. We are at the half way point. It is the darkest, most narrow spot in the alley-like walk to the river. I know this place. There is directly behind Mr. Cartwright, a smeared red gash of a stain on the cave's wall, a hieroglyphic of sorts, a desperate handprint no one ever sees, that no one ever stops to witness. But I know it is there.

"You don't know what you will be up against. I have allies in the local government. You will need me!" I say.

He sighs. I imagine him begging for forgiveness. I see him hanging. I am flying with the drug.

"This is not the time or place for this. I'm done." he says.

It is too dark, at this point, to see. In a few feet, there is a sharp curve, another lantern, a path toward the river. But we are not there yet. I step closer and I can smell the stink of him, the cheap sailor's cologne, the sweating despite the cool, a hint of whisky.

"You don't fool me Cartwright," I say. "I can squash your deal. Snopes own this town. We have for a century."

To punctuate my threat, I press the toe of my shoe into the floor and ceremoniously grind. I feel an energy rising in my chest, a light flaring from my eyes. He shall cower, and in the dull gray light there are shadows, there are nesting bats and I glimpse the phantom of Daddy swaying yet still alive neck broken lips quivering guiding me.

"I will take care of you like my father took care of yours. We Snopes know how to handle the likes of you."

"What did you say," he shouts. "You don't know anything about my father, you lunatic. I told you never to mention his name again. I'll box your ears right here and now."

I step closer more. "You are nothing in this city. Go back to Chicago. You don't belong here, Cartwright!"

I feel big grubby hands at my chest, a wrenching shove and a dark growl. I teeter back, and fall.

"You are nothing but a stupid brute," I scream.

He is moving away, cursing, bumping the walls, making his way up and out. "Stay away from me," he yells, his voice blotted, distant in the vague hollows of this cave, this place of mine. "You damned madman."

I sit and wait for him to leave. I am cool and comfortable here, in this darkest place, that handprint weak and useless still reaching out, still clawing with the vain ambitions of men like Cartwright, so easily broken. I smile, then lie back on the cool stones. I can hear Daddy's laughter.

# SEVENTEEN

*Drunk at Planter's bar. Meeting with Calhoun.*

*Clement Cartwright*

I'VE GOT A ringside seat at the swanky Planter's House Hotel bar. It has become a regular haunt for me during my stay here in St. Louis. I'm drinking to wash off the stink of Belasco Snopes. A small crowd gathers to watch the bartender, Jerry "Olympus" Thomas set whiskey on fire then toss that flaming stuff between two mixing glasses.

"Behold the Blue Blazer," Jerry shouts.

He's a stout man with a weightlifter's physique and a dandy's glitter. His tight suit, a bright-yellow cotton, looks ready to bust with each move, biceps straining. He wears a blue scarf and diamond stickpin at the throat, plus gems on every finger and sparkling cuff links. A painted advertisement, done up during his stint at San Francisco's Occidental Hotel features him in a bright gold cape surrounded by flames.

"Give her a try, gents." Jerry passes around glasses.

Light applause and the men disperse, leaving me to my gin and solitude.

"Another Tom Collins?" Jerry says.

I nod while he stirs up his own creation of gin, lime and lemon. I've been sizing up the place. It's a large semi-circle, a good design for a wide and windowless space. The door-less front entry spills out into the hotel's lobby with its colored marble walls and a grand central staircase featuring a pair of bronze lamp-holding sprites on the newel posts. I've been sketching on a napkin, a series of ideas for the St. Nicholas, which will become the Planter's competition a few blocks away. Jerry sets out my drink. I wonder if we could hire him away when the St. Nicholas opens. I wonder if Snopes will be crazy enough to try to sabotage our plan.

"There's an odd one," he says, pointing to the entrance, then turning to the mirror lining the bar's back wall to fuss with his scarf.

I nod and take a look. The young ruffian from the river hovers. A thrill runs up my spine. I haven't seen him since that night. I gave up on him, but looks like he found me. He's dressed in the same torn pants I'd seen him in last, though his shirt is clean and his hair is slicked. I wave to him and he slinks over, slowly, hesitatingly.

"You know that one?" Jerry says.

"He's down on his luck looking for work I imagine," I say.

"Been there myself. Worked the minstrel shows for a good while before finding my calling behind a bar," Jerry says, still at the mirror.

He stands near me head lowered yet looking up at me from beneath his furrowed brow. I grasp his hand and shake it fiercely. It's big, strong and callused, so unlike Snopes, that moneyed softness, that weak grip. I do not let go of his hand, and he does not pull away and our eyes stay on one another and it is in this moment that I realize what he is, what he could be to me. There is always a point of pure instinct for men like me, a brief fire of knowing.

"I'm glad you finally came," I say softly.

He smiles, and I release my grip.

"I got a good spell of work at the brewery. I can't turn down money. I been meaning to come," he says. "My name's Calhoun, you'd mentioned you was staying here at the hotel."

"Jerry show him the Blue Blaze, it's on me."

I am invigorated and unabashedly happy. Calhoun stands near me and I drape my arm across his wide shoulders. I can smell his cheap hair tonic. I am struck by a fierce sense of kinship. There's a smell to him, of earth, and I think of my hands on him that night at the river and I know I should calm down, should step away but it is all to intoxicating and I let myself get riled another moment before I finally remove my arm.

Jerry's diamonds reflect the amber glow of the fiery whiskey, a torrent of movement as he shakes and tosses the liquor. He sets the drinks down, along with two beers.

"Let her cool." Jerry turns to take care of a group of college men in derbies.

We are standing close, and I keep my arm over his shoulder.

"Jerry," I yell. "You still looking for help?"

Jerry leans across the wide mahogany bar and sizes up Calhoun. "This one?" he says, looking from me to Calhoun.

"Can you lift a case or two?"

"I work nights at Snopes, hauling," Calhoun says. "Would be grateful to get out of that place."

"Show me your hands," Jerry says.

Calhoun lays them on the bar. Jerry grabs them, flips them over, lets them go.

"Like an ape," he says. "I need someone a few nights a week to haul liquor and bus glasses. You'd need to clean up and wear a suit."

"We can get that done," I say.

"He a poor relation?" Jerry asks. "Or you working for the missions now, Mr. Cartwright?"

"Give us two of your gin drinks," I say.

Calhoun turns to me. "I'm most grateful, sir."

"Clement, call me Clement," I say.

"All right."

Holding my eyes, his lips curl less in a smile than a snarl, a beastly thing, a few teeth visible, a wild revealing that is at once arresting and sublime. He is quite a specimen.

"I need somebody to show me this city. I want to see it how I used to remember it." I pick up my gin. "Back before I got soft."

He lifts his drink and downs it in one lick, then slams the glass down in a clumsy way. I can see in his soft, steady gaze a reflection of nights lost at that river alone, so many nights, before I found my way out of St. Louis and off to discover the man I would become.

"Let's go to my room for a whiskey," I say.

He hesitates, then gets up slowly and moves away. I follow knowing we have both without words begun stepping into a dark alley of unknowing, a leap of trust, a possible disaster as we head up to my room for the night.

# PART TWO

# EIGHTEEN

*A dream. Lunch at Edna's. Belinda's wedding. Mr. Snopes, a devouring man.*

*Dolores Brattridge*

A YOUNG MAN is naked and wet at the foot of my bed. A petal shaped scar stretches across his stomach and he is smeared with dirt and I ask, "Is that from the river or from my garden?"

"Why did you let me go?" he says in a voice I recognize as Charles'.

I struggle with the question, and then think of our lost child, our only child. I have always blamed myself, my weakness and frailty for losing what Charles wanted so much, for that miscarriage. That of course was when I began the laudanum.

There is a weak knock at the bedroom door and I shake myself awake, pulling away from the dream and the drowsy netherworld of phantom regrets. A kitchen maid deposits an urn of coffee. Where is Claire? Who is this young thing in a bonnet? I sit up but cannot dispel the dream. I am disheartened and afraid being alone so much since Charles left. My fainting spells are worse. I am not eating. But I also know my truth, that without Charles' reassuring presence, my mind becomes more my own, my ideas scatter wildly, and my premonitions, those things I have always know since I was a girl, they announce themselves more clearly and more often.

"You have the curse," Mother told me long ago. "Or the blessing. Your Aunt Awilda had it, so blame her, dear. But it is wonderful when one loses a brooch."

Secretly, I think of it as witchery, this pre-knowing, this seeing certain truths others are blind to. I do not know how, but I am certain I will encounter the young man from my dream. But I won't think of it now. I must dress and prepare to go to Edna's.

She has invited me to join Belasco Snopes and his sister Belinda for lunch at her home in Lafayette Square. We will discuss the girl's upcoming wedding. Belinda, a fragile and charming young woman with wide bright eyes and hair the color of sun-paled cherries, has become dear to both of us.

Despite her wealth and advantages, Belinda has always worried me. Since turning sixteen, she has spoken to me on several occasions, in hushed tones, short vibrating sentences in private, confessing her growing fear of her brother, her desire to untangle from what she calls "the family curse of melancholy." Then last spring, she came to me flushed and excited, sharing the news that she had accepted an offer of marriage from Heinrich Schuller, heir to the German brewing empire. I sat her down.

"It's a smart union," Belinda said quickly. "Since father's death, we need this. It's the right thing. Did you know the Schuller brewery staff ties tiny blue ribbons around each bottle of beer? Isn't that wonderful? Thousands of ribbons. They started their business in Germany and are going to open a factory in Milwaukee. Isn't that something?"

She was wearing pink that afternoon. The pale silk crept up her neck blending with her soft complexion and famous red hair, creating an image nearly too startling to take in. She had looked over her shoulder several times, though we were alone in my room that day. I knew she was frightened.

"Do you love him?" I took her hands in my own.

She faced me and remained very still. I noticed a tiny white flower petal hidden in the froth of her crimson hair as if she had rushed through a hedge on her way.

"Do you?"

With her sitting, so still, so close, I saw a delicate cut on her left ear with but a scant drop of blood.

"I have to get away." She glanced repeatedly over her shoulder. "There are things I have never told you about Belasco."

We had been interrupted before I could touch that cut, ask her more, but today I hope to pull her aside, to stroll with her through the garden, to ask her about that day and more, to ask her to tell me the truth about Schuller and the wedding and of course, her brother Belasco.

I dress, order my carriage and arrive at Edna's a bit early still in a partial haze from my restless night and my strange dreams. A servant leaves me alone on the second-floor patio overlooking the back garden, which is as chaotic as it is pristine. Edna has mixed the most exotic blooms, black dahlia next to marigold and lilies, these thrusting forth to stab neatly clipped hedges. A beautiful disaster, her garden.

In my mind it is the undeniable warmth in Edna's intentions that keeps her above the fray of gossip, despite her unusual life choices. Others insist it is her title, Countess Panzutti (a title she refuses to use, though people use it for her).

"Things are so much greener after a storm," Edna says, joining me. "I love the assault to the senses."

There are bristling voices from below. I hear Belinda and secretly wish she were coming alone. I do not care for Belasco Snopes. He is always impeccably dressed and has a fine way of speaking, but he reminds me of a ferret with his piercing eyes and dark, probing manner. His speech is clever, but I do not believe he says what he actually means. I will focus on Belinda's warmth. We turn from the patio table and Belinda accosts us with a rush of yellow, her dress an absolute reflection of this glowing day.

"Dolores," she says.

Our cheeks touch, then our hands. Hers are trembling and cold. In her eyes I see what I have seen before, the look of someone fleeing. Her brother Belasco is behind her wearing a checked suit of a heavy fabric, despite the heat, and his hair has a great amount of sheen.

"You are the only man I know who will come to lunch," Edna says as Benedict, a lanky and very fair, young servant emerges from downstairs, on the ready.

Belasco has taken the seat directly across from me. His penciled lips are squeezed tightly shut. I imagine a forked tongue slipping out to snatch an insect.

"I do what I need to in order to support my sister." He pulls a black handkerchief from his pocket and gently dabs his narrow forehead. "She is foolish."

Belinda, whose bright hair hangs as a world of loose curls, laughs. "Soon enough I will be off of your hands," she says.

"Is that what you think?" Snopes says, pocketing his handkerchief. "You will never be truly away from us. You are a Snopes after all."

"Family is family, yes." Edna nods. "Let's have champagne, Benedict. With raspberries to start. And pudding."

The sunlight is momentarily diffused by a thin veil of a cloud, and I suddenly, and without reason, find that I cannot look away from Belasco, who I am sure is studying me. As Edna speaks of the wedding, the sun re-emerges directly behind him, shining on his back, curling around him and casting a shadow toward us. I think: It is as if he is a bit of night, a rush of the dark, not even of this season, as if the sunlight cannot bear him, cannot touch him so it sluices around him entirely, flailing out in other directions, harmed. Belasco is harming the light, I think.

I look away, knowing that my mind is not mine. I am fatigued, and I blame it on Charles, on his absence. I recall my dream and looking at Belasco I am struck with a premonition that something terrible is going to happen. Something that has to do with the architect, Mr. Cartwright.

Edna mentions the wedding flowers and Belinda laughs and I think: I have not had such thoughts since a girl, not since I was Belinda's age when there were long stretches of stray mangled imaginings that overtook me in the dawdling Mediterranean sun. Those summers, even in crowds, odd instincts and visions of things I knew would come to be. All of this, my sudden and horrible fascination with the light and memories of the past overwhelms me.

Belasco is watching me again, and I see a black outline that is his visage and I see the light withering and I hear Edna and I must come back to myself. He is about to speak, to begin a web of conversation that I fear could draw me closer to some sudden madness so I speak quickly and with distinction.

"I am so happy to host the wedding breakfast of course," I say.

Benedict is serving a flaming pudding with the champagne. The flames of the pudding, slowly diminishing, are rising before Snopes and all light has gone and I say to myself, *enough Dolores, that is enough. You are a grown woman not a girl flailing in the waves.*

"It's a wonderful idea," Edna says. "Belinda has no women in that household and you cannot count on your ailing Aunt Lorraine from the East to take it on. Dolores will do a marvelous job."

"It's not really correct, she's not family." Snopes digs a spoon into the pudding's fleshy top coating. "But it can't be helped."

"I thank you, Dolores," Belinda says softly, her hand on mine, that gentle touch releasing me from my passing hysteria.

"Do you know much of Mr. Cartwright?" Snopes says.

I am grateful the topic has turned. "He is quite a success…"

"Did you know he was building a hotel near the Planter House Hotel, and that he and a partner are opening an office in St. Louis? You were the first to host him at a dinner. I presume you know more than most."

There is a mild wind and I smell the sea, which is impossible, it is only the river. Oysters replace the pudding.

"I am afraid I know very little," I say.

"I thought it was a lady's duty to know her guests. Cartwright, who was raised in abject poverty here, in absolute obscurity, now calls himself not just an architect but an artist, a painter, a poet. I read he sculpted a bust of Austin Pendleton," Snopes says, shucking and scooping. "A bust!"

The oysters are on my plate but I cannot tolerate raw fish. And there in the breeze is the sea, that Mediterranean summer, that girl I was. *Be gone. Be gone.*

"The British author, that Pendleton, how unusual," Edna says.

"Uncanny and preposterous! Any man who tries to succeed at too many things fails at all. And yet here he is taking over projects in our city," Snopes says. "And why does he hide his past? What else is he hiding I ask you ladies? He comes from the sewer if I can be so bold. His father worked at our brewery and was thrown out. A thief. He seems unnaturally committed to bachelorhood—"

Belinda, who has never let go of my hand, cries out, "Please, Belasco!" There is raggedness to her cry which startles us all. "Please," she says again more softly.

"It's the oysters," says Edna. "They are making us all raving mad. What was I thinking? Please forgive me. Let's turn back to the wedding breakfast."

Edna is up, calling to her man, asking for a soup and more champagne.

"Clement Cartwright is not to be trusted, that's all I am saying and everyone should know that," Snopes says. "He is not one of us. And I intend to reveal him for what he really is and send him scampering back to Chicago after the Landsworth building opens."

A soup has arrived with a clatter and Edna guides us out of the gloom, back to next spring and joyful wedding predictions. I am listening, and slowly contribute, but cannot shake a feeling that I have unwittingly set a tide in motion, a tattered bit of gloom that had no business here today, an insight that would have been better left buried. Mother once told me that there are roots better left hidden deep under red, black earth, bits in life that ought never to be brought into the sunlight. Charles had steadied me but he is gone now. I know that it is my doing, my secret madness, but I know too, watching Belasco Snopes dip his finger to test the heat of a clear soup, I know he is a devouring man to be reckoned with. I have a part in it all, of that I am sure.

# NINETEEN

*Poker. Back to the river. Going West.*

*Calhoun McBride*

FAT FRANK GOT us in a poker game with a group of river rats plus one real-live dandy who calls himself Mr. Farrow. Farrow's in town for the Landsworth building opening. How he found his way to us I can't figure. He's got an icy sick-pale look and he's wearing a heavy suit in the high heat. He's got a high-pitched laugh and pockets full of money.

We been playing since midnight. I'm down, but hoping I might lay out a royal flush this hand if the cards sing for me, if my one-eyed friend Jack comes calling. Farrow goes real slow on his turn, telling stories that go nowhere. Since he's losing, nobody gives two shits.

"Landsworth building gonna pierce the sky fellas, gonna start a new revolution and this gut-stinking little city will bust open. Do you know that? Do you all know what we are witnessing here! But I'll tell you one who ain't so happy. Belasco Snopes. He'd be happy to tear that building down, to run that Cartwright out of town. I seen him down here by the river, sniffing around, looking for trouble. But then he can do what he pleases. He owns this town!"

His voice rises high and his eyes all but roll back in his skull and I wonder if he's eaten solid food in short of a week. I keep praying for my one-eyed jack. I draw and there's the old red queen staring at me, laughing.

"Out," I say, laying down my cards.

Fat Frank stays in. Guy I call curly and another old cuss hold tight, too, and it's back to Farrow and he's betting big. The more he loses, the higher he bets. I'm wondering if it's a sin to take advantage of a man clearly half baked. But then I think how the gold on his fingers alone could get me out of St. Louis and off West by morning, so I can't feel too bad. He calls and there it is.

"My four friends, gentlemen. Look at them," Farrow says.

There's my one-eyed jack. Matter of fact he's got all four jacks and takes that hand easy. Maybe he ain't gonna lose all night after all. Fat Frank cuts loose a long low sigh. He ain't done so well. Farrow racks in his winnings then hops up and we all jump a little, thinking he might pull out a revolver.

"I have to go, gentlemen. I have more to see this brilliant night."

Normally, you can't win and run, but being he lost all night and most of us made out pretty damn good, we all stay quiet and wait for him to make his way, still talking, moving fast and wild away from the table. Door wheezes open and shut and I catch the river's scent and Fat Frank stands up, stretching like a bear.

"That it for me," he says.

The rest grumble and we all start to move out. I follow Fat Frank and we head for the river. It's cooler there. He's likely to have a bottle with him under one of them layers of fat.

"Fixing to rain again," I say, as we settle close to the shore.

River's quiet, boats docked until dawn's bustle.

Fat Frank settles, passes me a bottle. "Think so?" he says.

The river's high. Been raining pretty steady, not enough to flood, but it's getting near. Frank's been through a few bad floods. He was working on the Memphis Belle when she got smacked hard, tossed in a storm and smashed to pieces. Fat Frank's seen things. Lost folks. There's a way he stares out the river like he can see the past.

"When you go west?" he says. "You been seeing a lot of that Cartwright fella lately."

I pass the bottle back. Far off I hear a rumble. Sky looks clear but could be a storm scooting over from Illinois. They come up fast in summer.

"I been thinking," I say.

"Well there's your problem."

I don't get mad since he's right. Things ain't never gone too well when I tried to figure them out in my head. I'm better at just taking a leap. Like hopping off that Orphan train, or trusting Fat Frank. There's another rumble, softer this time so maybe the storms moving east. I wonder who the hell I'm gonna talk to out West.

"I'm thinking I best stick around awhile. I got good work at the Planter's House hotel bar. Mr. Cartwright set that up. I don't need to go back to the brewery. Plus, they're going all out with the Landsworth building grand opening at the end of the month. I hear there's gonna be fireworks."

"Thought you were fired up to get on?" Fat Frank says.

I take a quick side glance, trying to figure his angle but he's still got on his poker face. He don't turn to me, just keeps staring at the river. I can't think of nothing to say.

"Sounds like a good choice to me," Frank says. "You think you gonna ever meet anybody like that Mr. Cartwright out west?"

He holds my eye and I know what he's getting at. He's got a real gentle face if you take the time to look at it. He ain't never judged me harsh. He don't ask what I don't feel like telling. And I don't ask nothing about what he and Bessie got. There's parts of me I figured would always just stay quiet and cast off, like old bottles to the hungry mouth of the river. I never expected anything to change for me, never expected to get close to a man. Then Cartwright came along. And everything feels different.

"I'd guess not likely to meet a fella like that, no," I say.

Another rumble, closer now.

"Yeah it's coming. Another storm," Fat Frank says. "That ain't good, look at her, near to burst, that river. Can't hold too much more. You gonna want to look at what you got in front of you, Calhoun. You gonna want to take a good long look."

We both settle back. I take that in, the figuring Frank just done for me, the way he lays things out without saying anything, and I think them fireworks is gonna be something nobody with half a brain would want to miss, and I wonder where Cartwright is gonna be when all that is going on, since he's the one that came up with that building in the first place. It's his, in a way. Which is really something.

# TWENTY

*The gentlemen meet. A grand opening. Buildings rise, crumble.*

*Clement Cartwright*

THE RAIN HAS set in with force, long thrashing slags of it, heavy and relentless. It's been raining consistently all month. I have never seen a tempest of this caliber. A dark, masculine, walloping thing. Folks are talking about the great flood of 1874 wondering if we are headed for another disaster. Walking out of doors is to face its onslaught, hard bits of hail, and the sky disappearing under its weight. Between downpours, there are brief periods of calm. The sky is a landscape of mountainous clouds. Mammoth gray and low hanging as if half the river has been sucked up into their belly. These are the type of clouds that spit out tornadoes. The storm is a wild and thrilling thing and I yearn to be right smack inside of it, surrounded by its brutality and hungry force, off at the river's edge with Calhoun that rascal, swimming as my father never would have allowed.

We have gathered for a meeting in the study of Caldor Landsworth. I represent our architectural firm and further, Chicago. The rest are local men, including Snopes who slithered into the fold. I have not seen him since that ridiculous encounter at his brewery. His stake in the Landsworth building is not substantial; it is his importance in the city that brought him here today. The Landsworth Building opening party is at the end of the month. Despite the storms, the men are determined to have fireworks.

"She's swelled but it will be done soon, this storm can't last." Landsworth lights a cigar. "We won't have a flood. Mark my words."

He is a large man. Wide shoulders, big belly, a thick mass of dark hair and mutton chop sideburns. He has always struck me as a kind and educated fellow, as someone you wouldn't mind taking a long train ride with. His wealth and power have not ruined him. My collar is soaked, not from the rain, but from the horrible humidity. I tug at it.

"Not used to our tropical summers anymore, Cartwright?" Snopes says.

His fascination with me has not lagged since our first meeting several weeks ago. It has, in fact, worsened. He seems relentless in getting his way. Or he may be flat out crazy.

"The fireworks, the beer tent, it will bring the public in," says a nervous fellow named Hector Farrow. "Pacify the riff-raff. Make for a real grand event!"

Farrow, a wily investor from New York City is wide-eyed, well-dressed, very pale, very rich and excessively reliant on alcohol and poker games, that is what Landsworth says of him in private. He has a wild way about him which I find appealing. They say he lingers amidst the river folk, slinking about late at night. I think momentarily about Calhoun. I've told him to come to my room at the Planter's House hotel later tonight. We have been seeing each other often.

"The good thing about a flood is it cleanses the trash on the riverfront," says Snopes. "Our city cannot abide what lives down there. Those shacks and derelicts. St. Louis is on the verge of greatness we can't be yanked down. We need to control all of that." Snopes' voice rises with excitement. "Don't you agree Cartwright? You pulled yourself up out of that muck. You know it better than any of us."

Farrow chuckles then there is a stillness—that gentle lacing of rain across the lawn, a hush—then a sudden thrash of wind and a crackle of lightning. The men are looking toward me. Landsworth re-lights a fat cigar.

"There is life in the river," I begin. "Great possibility and a thrill of the indefinable, the sort of thing that can inspire a man. Being of water and earth. Have you swum the river Snopes? Have you gotten close to it, that thing that brings those barrels of beer, the commerce we all thrive on? Have you touched the shore?"

His pinched face has taken on a look of what appears to be terror, but holding his eye, I see it is quiet rage. He steps toward me, fists slowly clenching.

"Have you?" he says.

He is near me and he smells of licorice and his breath is hot and foul.

"Yes, I have. I still swim in the river. It's what this city is all about," I say. "If you bother to get to know and understand it."

He steps back as if the soul of the river, the dirt of it could disease him. His eyes go wide. "You swim that river alone? Foolish with the rip current."

The men wait. I am bold.

"A local young man showed me a good spot. I can take you there sometime. But maybe you don't know how to swim."

There is mild chuckling.

Landsworth hoists himself up, sucking the cigar, its tip flamed and snapping. "All right, gentlemen, and I use that term loosely today," he says.

"We've got a building to open by the end of the month. Enough about the river and this storm. We've seen much worse. Clement is an artist, an eccentric which is why I hired his firm. He has created a building that will be remembered in perpetuity. And it has my name on it! Now what of the party after the ribbon cutting gentlemen? I hear we have a jazz singer."

"Marvelous! St. Louis knows its jazz," says Farrow, standing and moving quickly toward the bar. "Where's the fellow with the champagne?"

I drift to a window, that fascinating onslaught of rain. To step out into it, to drench myself, to run through the hail dripping with Calhoun in my arms. I can taste him.

Landsworth raises a glass. "To our grand achievement gentlemen! The night before the ribbon cutting party, I want you all here. We will have a private affair. With some very special entertainment."

Snopes tilts back on his heel and sucks in a breath. When he begins to speak, he is interrupted by a deafening crash of thunder.

We are all momentarily silent, and I sense a fearful recognition of the might of nature, the power of what is not acknowledged amidst our lofty expectations and our man-made self-importance, our buildings that can at once rise, and so easily crumble.

# TWENTY-ONE

Twombly. The state of business. A chance encounter with Calhoun.

*Belasco Snopes*

BRADFORD TWOMBLY IS a spineless fleck of a man. I could whisper this in his ear, stand up and smack him with my glove and he would only lower his head and wait. To me he is a necessary bore.

He is a bachelor, thin to the point of emaciation, and white as chalk. In extreme contrast to his sickliness, he has a rich head of golden hair as well as an uncanny talent for numbers. His father was our family accountant for decades, and when he passed on from tuberculosis, his son, Bradford, took over. We are the same age, Bradford and I.

I have hated him since childhood, distrusted his constant bookish shyness, his poor health and ghostly appearance. I despised him even more when my father, one Christmas when the Twomblys came to dinner, had compared the boy to me. "The two of you could be twins," Daddy had said.

"Both sickly and weak."

After dinner, when the adults had left us boys alone in my room, I told Twombly we were going to play a special game. I blindfolded him, tied his hands together (something I had seen Daddy do in the factory, late one night, to a whimpering young woman) then I had beat the back of his legs with a stick. Before I untied him, I told him if he ever spoke of this I would come to his worthless little cottage late at night and kill him. I told him he was never to imagine himself in the same light as me, that I was his superior no matter what my father said.

Later in life, when he took over for his father and we met as men, I knew looking into his narrow, frightened little eyes, that he had never forgotten that episode. When it comes to reporting the financials of our brewery, however, Bradford Twombly, like his father, is uncommonly fearless, honest and sharp.

"You ought to move up the wedding date, to gain traction on the merger with Schuller," Twombly says his thin white fingers fidgeting with a stack of papers. "These latest reversals. It's all going to come to light. And we can't stall some of these gambling debts. If only we hadn't lost the St. Nicholas deal."

We are in the Turkish Den, a lounge of the Planter's House Hotel, sequestered in an elaborately brocaded, tasseled corner with mirrored walls. I can see myself looking at Bradford, and I see both him and the duplicate of him in the mirror, hunched and nervous. I imagine my reflection beating him about the head until something golden ekes out of his number rattled brain. I am enjoying an absinthe cocktail spiced with cinnamon.

"I will talk to my sister, but Schuller is a beast. If he senses we are up to something he will sniff it out," I say. "You need to hold things together a while longer. I haven't given up on getting into the St. Nicholas and being part of that capital share. I blame you for not being privy to that deal."

Twombly lifts his head slowly. We have worked closely since my father's death, since I took over managing our ailing brewery. He knows my vices, my truths, my methods. He even knows of Jenny Claire.

"I don't see how you can manage that," he says quietly. "I wasn't aware of Cartwright's reach. His man Ramsey is crafty and they have a lot of strong ties here in St. Louis. They are only getting stronger."

I smile and lift my drink, draining it. Coming across the room, past a backless couch covered in a brilliant blue azalea patterned fabric is a tall, dark haired young oaf that I have seen before, but cannot quite place. He is dressed in a shoddy serving suit, carrying a crate and moving swiftly. He passes near us and it comes to me. He is a drab who has worked at my brewery. I decide to have a bit of fun with him.

I wave to the young man. "You, wait a minute." The absinthe has begun its gentle caress. I can breathe more easily. "You work at my brewery do you not? Why are you here?

I can sense some fragrant breeze, and I notice in the golden tiles on a nearby fireplace mantle the formation of a face. I must not allow myself to drift. The absinthe is a delicious brew.

"I work here," he says.

"Traitor," I say, conjuring ways to get under the oaf's skin. "What did you do to get this job you dirty drab!"

"Mr. Cartwright got me the job fair and square." He is shifting side to side, nervous, sweaty, his arms swelling with the weight of the crate. He holds it, cradles it with much care, as if it were a sickly lamb.

"Cartwright?" I say.

In the pause, the boy continues on his way.

"How charitable of Mr. Cartwright," I say. "To find work for the unfortunate."

"I think we should pay off Cutler. The poker losses. They are manageable and we don't want him making a fuss," Bradford says.

"He's a boil on this city's ass," I say. "He's a pimp and a dirty dealer."

"He's stupid and wily. If Schuller were to find out you are in any way associated with that type, any of those undesirables from the river, it won't bode well. We don't want anything to give the Schuller's reason to back out," he says.

"It's a wedding. My sister believes it's about love," I say, motioning to the waiter for another drink. "You worry too much."

Twombly, like most men breathing, feel a fondness for my sister. Poor, feeble-minded Belinda. Gentle and soft, that petal she, long ago crushed under the feet of we Snopes men. Just like my poor mother. I see Twombly's lips quivering; he is searching for the right words to convince me. His presence is an irritation.

"I will talk to Belinda about the wedding. And that stuck up Mrs. Brattridge who is throwing the wedding breakfast and serving as my sister's confidante. She is an idiot but well respected. I'll get her on our side somehow," I say. "I'm going to stay, you may go."

Twombly shuffles his papers and stands, nods and leaves me to my fresh drink. The lug with the crate has crossed the lounge again and is conferring with a man up front. They are shaking hands and I leave money on the table, waiting for the boy to leave, then I follow.

The lug is lumbering across the lobby rotunda, which is quite grand. The cathedral height ceilings are decorated with medallions of choice heraldic design. An immense staircase, which he is climbing, is topped by a huge bronze guardian lion, which in my very mild delirium is salivating.

I trail the young man by several feet, and once he turns down a hall, I witness his entry to a room at the hall's end. I stand at that door, listening, but there is silence. Then I hear voices, hear whispers, hear things I can piece together.

At the lobby desk, I easily secure the information I need. The room in question, a suite, belongs to Mr. Clement Cartwright.

# TWENTY-TWO

A wet afternoon. A scandlous book. Mr. Snopes is lonely.

*Dolores Brattridge*

EDNA AND I are making the best of a wet afternoon. It has been raining on and off all month. We are perched side by side on my bed. There is tea and the open window brings a scent that is rich with earth, that scent which emerges after a storm. The fragrance is gentle, yet secretly disturbs me.

"Are you worried about Charles?" Edna asks.

I had not thought of Charles and am ashamed. I try to shape my thoughts and there is a desire to give in, to unravel a certain disquiet that I have not yet been able to put into words. Edna casts a spell on me; she makes me feel so young when we are alone, as if nothing is sacred and anything possible.

"I dislike Mr. Snopes. He is a terrible man," I say.

"Is that what you were thinking?"

"No." I had been thinking of Mr. Cartwright, bothered by a growing sense that something terrible is already in motion. "I'm undone Edna," I say, and I cannot stop the tears.

She pets me. "I am shocked that you do not cry more often. You suffocate yourself here. You are so much more, my dear, and this summer there is a chance to fulfill that."

Our eyes meet. She will not look away and there is such wisdom there.

There is a book circulating in St. Louis, written by a socialite, a story of a woman's awakening, of her desire for another man, of her trajectory away from her husband but toward herself. It has caused a minor scandal and the writer, that woman, is ruined.

"Don't be so dramatic, Dolores. I suggest you get out more often. That you go with me to the Opera. That you admit you hate Mr. Snopes, and that you allow yourself to breathe."

I am ashamed and question my own thoughts, my own devious subconscious. Things have unraveled since Charles' departure. I feel coiled. I shut my eyes and lean my head on Edna's strong shoulder.

"What do you think makes Mr. Snopes so wicked? I fear he is bent on ruining Mr. Cartwright whom I rather like."

"He is terribly lonely, and that enrages him. It enrages most men. They cannot tolerate the feeling, though we can and are expected to. He will never admit it. He will ruin men with his devious plots. He will find pleasure in another's demise. But it will only enflame the wound. Men are such children. You know that better than I."

I recall running to Edna early in my marriage, when Charles had thrown out my easel and paints, when he had refused my request to summer in Europe, when he had laid down his own particular laws. That feels so terribly long ago.

"What will you wear to the Landsworth party? Come and show me," Edna says. "It's out of doors, I have no clue. I haven't even begun to plan my look."

She has gone to open the window wider, and then into my dressing chamber. I do not move until she calls for me again, and then I go.

# TWENTY-THREE

*Fireworks are coming. A Landsworth affair.*

*Clement Cartwright*

THE PARTY BEFORE the party, the explosion of ego before the ribbon cutting fireworks tomorrow night—this is an evening I have dreaded all month.

The Landsworth estate's ballroom has been transformed with cavernous lighting, fur covered settee and ghastly mounted animal heads all meant to cast a hard, masculine edge of things hunted. But this is not the worst of it. The room is stifling, the only air provided by young scantily clad women with huge ceremonial fans, brushing the air around as if shooing flies. I do not move, think to turn slowly, to flee, to find Calhoun. He has visited me often this week, spending the night at my hotel. I got him a job at the grand opening night party, a chance to have him near me. He fills my mind often. I down a glass of scotch and wait.

Snopes is watching me from an outer edge of the large oval shaped room. He leans on a piano. Caldor Landsworth has burst out of shadow with two pale, half nude women on his arm, ruddy faced and loud.

"There you are, Cartwright! We've got a show starting. This is the night to cut loose. Tomorrow will be all ceremony. Tonight, we are reckless. Here take this." He thrusts one of the pale women at me, this one white haired carrying a large white feather fan, draped in some sheer and shimmering get up.

"Get over near the piano, that's where the action is," Landsworth says, moving back into the false night he came from.

I tell the white feathered woman to go and get herself a drink. I avoid the piano, where Snopes is holding court, waving his claw-like hands like a hysterical bird in distress.

I cross the room and end up jammed near a make shift group of dancers, women pale as ice in the terrible heat. The room is getting more and more crowded with men, Landsworth at the tip of it all, near those chilly looking girls all curvy, pale and glittery. I spot a stairway at one edge of the ballroom, and head there, sneaking up away from the ruckus.

There is a darkened balcony between floors, a mezzanine of sorts, overlooking the expanse of drunken men. It will be my oasis. The ballroom's maddening lack of light keeps the balcony in deep shadow. It wraps the circumference of the mighty room. It is narrow, with a few feet of marble on which to stand and a thin black railing offering a view to the hijinks below. There is a wall of books, mostly scarlet-colored, behind me, that also circles the room.

The golden women are dancing lasciviously, the men howling. Huge fans swing about. It has the appearance of a jungle gone mad, the black, oiled and shimmery tops of men's heads, the slick white-haired woman and those tribal feathered stalks. Things momentarily go quiet. Landsworth is saying a few words. Trays are circulating with champagne and I wonder if he will notice me gone. The jazz quartet has not quit playing, so his words are muffled. The crowd cheers and I step back toward the book case behind me, suddenly afraid of being spotted. There is another voice near me, an undeniable voice.

"I knew you were a coward," Snopes says. "Hiding in the shadows."

It is dark and I cannot yet see him, barely make out his droopy outline as he comes toward me from the stairs.

He speaks in a clear yet new and darker tone, punctuating each word and imbuing phrases with what feels like a terrible vileness. His words have taken on a hard angle, a low growling quality, a near ferociousness. I still cannot see him but I hear his steps, slow and deliberate. I grip the edge of a book, overcome with an odd sensation that he has come to harm me. I need to push past him to escape this ridiculous scene.

"You and I are similar in some ways," he says. "We let nothing stop us."

With that, I know he is near, and then I make him out fully as a bold artificial spotlight pops brightly from below, some climax to the cacophony, giving me a clear glimpse of Snopes. He is ghastly. The streak of momentary light casts a white glow to his face and his eyes are very wide, his mouth open and in his hand a tumbler of whiskey. His tie is gone and his shirt undone at the top. He is beginning to smile as the light disappears.

"I knew the day you arrived," he says. "I know what you are. I know. Drink with me."

Now he is upon me and he thrusts the tumbler at me for a drink. I move quickly to get past him on the narrow balcony but he will not budge, instead, he presses the hard glass tumbler at my lips and feeds me the liquor.

"Get out of my way," I shout.

This stalls him for a moment, and in that moment comes another flash of light and a hoot from the crowd as a high tremulous voice begins to sing a song in French. In that light I again see his face, which has become even more grotesque, and he is trembling. I notice how thin the balcony railing is, how easily it could snap.

"Come on," he says. "Come on!"

He has forced me against the bookcase, assaulting my lips with the liquor. I can easily box his ears but I fear my punch would send him right over the bannister into that mad crowd below. I open my eyes wide, see his black irises and the rage there and my rage and I tear away, thrust myself toward the railing which shivers as if to break. But it does not.

Snopes has turned to face the books, he is in slow motion, moving to a kneeling position and before he can turn back I hurry away to the staircase and down, through that disastrous party, overcome with disgust and a sense of irreproachable violation, off to the only chance for baptism, for cleansing, to find my Calhoun.

# TWENTY-FOUR

*A lingering dream. A walk to the gates. Calhoun.*

*Dolores Brattridge*

I HAD LAIN down, the bedroom window open, only a moment, never intending to sleep the afternoon away. Naps, a luxury of my youth, now leave me restless, unfocused. They are dangerous for me, Charles says. He forbids them.

There is a pungent scent of the river carried in with the evening wind. It is a sensual smell, rich like my garden at dawn after a rain but terrible, too, as if there is something deadly in it, something heavy and not alive. I sit up. It is dim and I am still disturbed by a dreamy memory of the Mediterranean, that summer night and the boy named Augustine. Charles knows of this childhood sweetheart of mine, but he does not know of the recurring dream, the Italian landscape that haunts me and that will not be shut away. I wonder if it is best to lie back down, to sleep through the night. I wonder, too, if the boy in the dream is at the same time my lost child, a remnant of that terrible time. It is all so strange.

The wind is strong and I allow the memory in, harmless really, a poem I had written which had made Augustine weep. He had not kissed me, but made me promise him something, had made me write this promise on a slip of blue paper, which sits folded under a false bottom in my main jewelry box, not touched for years. I know if I burn it the dream may vanish. So, I never have.

I force myself up, unable to remain in this netherworld of half sleep. I will dress and eat and have a glass of wine and things will brighten up. I make it to my window and the garden is spectacular. The wind animates it, lavender branches and midnight reds and oranges tangling and bending as if to break. There is a mild howl, some animal far off by the river. I put on soft shoes and make my way through the silent house, downstairs, through my sitting room, out to my garden. It will not be the first time I have wandered it at night. Charles sleeps like the dead.

It is surely going to storm again. I walk toward the archway, the porthole to my private place where Edna and I spend our time. The scent of the river, always pungent in our city, is particularly heavy tonight, as if the wind has scooped up muddy buckets as offerings to the clouds.

There have been times when I have gone further than my garden at night. I have stood at the threshold of our front door, usually watching guests leave. It has crossed my mind to wander out into the street toward those mighty Vandeventer gates, to watch a couple as they fade away. I have never done that. But Charles is not here; the servants have dimmed their lights and are hidden away. As I near the archway, I turn back, move into my sitting room beyond it, to our front door. I open it slowly, silently.

Near the gates a figure hovers. I am afraid but continue out, thinking of the story by Henry James and those children, were they alive or ghosts? The boy is pale and motionless and with each step I lose that terrible fear. I forget the taboo, the horror of a woman alone at night. I can turn and see the open door of the house, the scant light bleeding there. As I approach he looks up and I see that like a frightened animal he will flee.

"Wait," I call.

He stiffens and I see he is flesh and blood, no phantom. But too, I see, he is more. It is his height which is my height, that wide brow so like Charles, skin pale like mine and he does not move so I can see in the hard and brutal moonlight that he is what my son would be, my lost child, that infant never seen, he is the age of that one and he is staring at me with longing. And I suddenly see how this all will unfurl, the part I will play because my insight, my curse, my soothsaying to the future has come fully back to life and I know I am part of his sordid destiny. I step closer.

He casts his head down. "Sorry to disturb you," he says. "I was just passing by. I'll get on now."

I stand near him and realize that if I were to keep walking I would leave Vandeventer Place.

"How far is the river, if you were to walk?" I say.

He squints as if trying to see me.

"What?" he says.

"You must live on the river with your mother," I say.

"I don't live anywhere," he says.

He is a hard, gangly young man but there is something soft and gentle, too. "Where is your family?" I say.

"I ain't got no kin, I'm making my own way," he says. "My ma died when I was born."

I know even more now why I came to him, how my dream would not be shaken, how it took itself further, out here, how it drew me. I am silent and this boy lifts his head, looks at me, both concerned and afraid and the blue paper unfolds and I cannot bear it, that scrawled writing of mine at fifteen faded now: *Do no lose yourself, Dolores.*

"I am sorry for your loss," I say, turning away.

I am not afraid that he will follow me. I imagine I have disturbed him more than he has me. I, the odd phantom wandering the night. The mad woman.

# TWENTY-FIVE

*A spider's web. Overheard in the hall. Defeat.*

*Belasco Snopes*

IT WAS NOT at all difficult to draw the fat little spider into my web this early afternoon. I considered every word, syllable and double meaning as I constructed my note to Cartwright. I wrote short gentle sentences, and then redrafted it with just the slightest hint of dread. Nothing too vulgar, just a thinly disguised threat, a definitive knowing. I imagined Cartwright's first raging reaction upon receiving my note, his face flaming red, and his big chest huffing like a beast. He would crumple the plain white paper with an instinct to toss it in the fire. Then he would pause, and reconsider the fine underside of each word, the whispering harm of truth. The possible brutal consequences. Then would come his slow simmering doubt. He would unfold it, would read it over, study the curl of my penmanship, the meaning of the purple blue ink, he would haggle with himself, and then come to me.

Indeed, here he is standing before me feigning bravado when I know he shivers with fear.

"You've got two minutes, then I will tell you what I think of your idle threats," Cartwright says standing at his chair, not even taking a seat. "I only came to shut you up once and for all."

I would like to stay in this place of my reigning, my supreme Snopes showmanship, because I know I have the spider cornered. But he is a hot-headed brute, so I will behave. No need for broken chairs, or broken bones.

"Please sit, I won't need more than a moment I promise. I know our last meeting didn't go well," I say.

This drab, this false artist, tall, broad and red headed, more a pale ogre from a fairy tale than a man, he is scarlet in the face, his meaty fists clutching the edge of the seat and I know he'd love to clock me but he does sit, he orders a drink, he stares me down and he waits.

I've chosen a table at the Planter's House Hotel bar. The scene of the crime, the beginning of his end.

"It was smart of you to stay here at this place, scope out the competition while you plan your new hotel," I say.

Cartwright can barely contain his anger. "I don't like you, Snopes, and I don't trust you. You said you were running to that newspaper hack Dartmouth with incriminating information. You made veiled threats against my character. I'm sure Landsworth himself would have told me to ignore you. But I always face my enemies head on. That is what my father taught me," he says, flushed in the face, ruddy and ugly.

A waiter sets down our drinks and I begin in a low, slow voice.

"It was right here, at this table that I unexpectedly found Calhoun. It makes it easy for me, really. Daddy always told me to seek a man's most repugnant defect, his most fatal flaw. Get under the skin of that, take an objective view, understand its power and with that you can rule the world."

Cartwright downs his drink but does not look away. I can see he is nervous. There is a mild twitch to his left eyebrow. His face is like stone otherwise.

"Stop the damn riddles," he says.

"Oscar Wilde, when he visited St. Louis in 1882 chose to stay at The New Southern Hotel. His speech was quite a success at the Mercantile Hall. You would have enjoyed it, I imagine."

Cartwright is withdrawing just slightly into his chair as if it could swallow him. He waves for a second drink. Within me there boils a river of triumph, a rushing sensation, that bracing air on the snout of the winning race horse as it presses so delicately through the blue ribbon.

"It's terrible, the row Wilde is in with the Marquis of Queensberry. The Marquis' son is about the same age as that Calhoun fellow wouldn't you say?"

The waiter returns, Cartwright downs his drink.

"I followed Calhoun from this hotel, up to your room. So, I know, you see. I heard. The hall was empty and I heard so much," I say. "And that dirty young man can easily be bought, that's terribly clear don't you think? What a brilliant scandal just as they open the Landsworth building."

Cartwright slams a fist on the table, heads turn. He is seething, such a lovely thing to behold.

"You have nothing on me. What do you really want? What are you getting at?"

"I don't need to get at anything. Nothing at all. Unless that's the route you'd like to take. What I really need is a proprietary stake in the Landsworth building, as well as in the new St. Nicholas Hotel. As I said when we met at my brewery, we will be partners. I am the heart and guts of St. Louis.

Nothing happens here, no success, without me."

It is first evident in the eyes when a man is beaten. It is both a startled and battered look. It is the look one has on learning of the death of a loved one. It cannot be disguised.

"I've worked it all out," I say, handing over the documents.

He is slunk down into the table as he reaches across and takes the papers. That bright hair, those broad shoulders, the entirety of what was Mr. Clement Cartwright, architect and hero, has fallen.

# TWENTY-SIX

*Meeting at Grubbs. A Fist fight.*

*Calhoun McBride*

CLOUDS HANG LOW. Soot is deep and dark enough to stain my skin. Late afternoon smog carries the scent of manure and slum rot. I feel every bit a grubby animal yanked through coal dust as I head to meet Clement at Grubbs Tavern. He said he had something to tell me before the big Landsworth building party tonight. I'm thankful to him for getting me a job there. The money's good. I hope we end up back at his hotel room by the end of the night. Grubbs is a low-down joint, not a tavern I'd expect a man like Clement to step into. Maybe he's tired of the fancy folks.

I get us a spot in the far corner, past the piano. The place is crowded with thieves and whores, a few fellas I know from card games, drunks, slammers, hangers on. The outside soot grimes up the table and beer mugs. Everything's heavy with the sweat and tired meanness of these men and women beat up by the day, getting off from the brewery or getting away from riverboat work. I look around for Bessie but don't catch her in the crowd. Fat Frank drinks at home but Bessie likes to step out now and again.

An old girl with a tattered nest of dyed blonde hair and too much makeup is at the piano, belting out a song about a yellow canary. She's loud and red in the face and folks are clapping, singing along, but when she gives me a wink and a long look I can see she's past wore out, she's done for. I get a hard chill up my back wondering how long I might last running like I do, how long I can survive in this city. I would of gone West already if I hadn't met Clement. I been wondering if he might go West with me, that dream feeling coming closer every day.

I see him come in. He stands at the door, checks a gold pocket watch in his breast pocket, lights a cigar. The blonde at the piano catches sight of him, too. She puffs out her chest, presses back her hair and smiles, likely thinking that he's come to save her. I want to go over and give her a shake and tell her that nobody can save a soul lost that bad.

I stand up and wave and he comes my way and the closer he comes the more I want to get at him. Every head turns as he takes his seat, and a few fellas I know smirk and spit. I'm shaking a little 'cause I been aching so much for this moment, to ask him to go West with me, to feel that something really is possible between us.

The greasy barkeep comes over and Calhoun orders two whiskeys. Our chairs are close. His mane of red hair is hanging shaggy in his face today and he ain't shaved yet for the party which seems funny. His shirt and waist coat are open wide and his undershirt is showing. I can see a nick on his neck where he must have cut himself. I want to touch his neck but I don't.

"Something has happened," he says.

"Let's go," I say quickly. "Let's stop at your hotel before the big night."

Him so close, the smell of him, I can't stand waiting. I need to get at him. I stand.

"No," he says. "Sit down. I need to explain something to you."

He says it in a low angry tone, not looking at me. He drags on his cigar and looks at the singer who's wailing now about a man named Bill.

"You can tell me at the hotel. Come on. This ain't no place for you. We still got time."

"We can't go there," he says in that same dark, low tone. "We can't be seen there."

I sit down.

"Drink your whiskey," he says.

I do.

"Snopes told me something today."

He stops and stares dead at me like he forgot where he was and who I was. He's got a look like he just woke up from a nightmare or that somebody whispered some terrible reckoning in his ear. He's gone pale and I wonder if he's sick. Then he turns away from me like he can't stand looking at me, watching the singer and speaking low and steady again.

"Things have changed for us," he says.

I stand up since I know what's coming. I get hot all over 'cause I been through this and worse before. The blonde is still singing but it's like time quit moving. I start to go but he grabs my arm hard and forces me back into my chair. I try to stand but he grabs my arm tight.

"You ain't gotta say anything else," I say. "You got what you wanted from me and you're done. I been a fool to think anything else."

He pulls his hand away and there's another look on his face that I can't figure. His eyes go wide and his lips pull apart and he bears his teeth and I reckon he means to wallop me. I stand up once more and so does he.

"Snopes knows. He followed you."

I suddenly can't stand to be near him, can't stand remembering what I'd walked in dreaming about, what I let myself think could ever for a split second be true for the likes of me. I gotta get away. I start to move and he pushes me back and my chair turns over and I start again and this time I push him back hard.

"Stop," he yells, grabbing me.

The singer goes quiet and the crowd turns to watch. He starts to push me to my seat and the feel of his hand on my arm, that touch that sets me off toward a thousand bits of wonder. It's all too much so I make a fist and punch him flat in the face. It stops him for only a second then he rushes at me, landing his big fists on my chest, slamming me to the wall while the crowd cheers. The blonde singer rushes over near us and Clement is coming at me again, but as fast as my rage came on its gone, slipped away, and I let myself fall to the floor, sitting at his feet, hating every last bit of him but wanting to wrap myself around his legs so he can't move, so we can't never move again, so this half-assed togetherness as ugly as it is can't disappear.

# TWENTY-SEVEN

*A grand ribbon cutting. The party. A carriage ride with Mr. Cartwright.*

*Dolores Brattridge*

"I WILL NOT traipse to the riverfront to watch the men blow things up, nor will you dear," Edna says quietly, discounting the fireworks to come. "This storm threatens flood but no one seems to care."

We are with a small elite cluster, part of a larger crowd that stretches several blocks, in front of the Landsworth building. Our clan is dressed for evening in our jeweled chiffons, awaiting the literal cutting of a ribbon by Mr. Belasco Snopes.

The majority of the crowd is behind us standing ear to ear, hands on their hips, men, women and children in dirty broad cloth, hungry and gawking. Mr. Cartwright is speaking at length, and though there has been an abatement in the storm, a hot wind continues. Phrases make their way, jumbled.

"And casting aside historic styles as inspiration...may use an original and modern style to attain visual unity," he says. "Ten stories, a human expression of a tall steel..."

Edna is restless. "Palazzo style, how modern, first of its kind as if that's a good thing. It houses the offices of the Brewers Association," she says, sighing and clutching my arm. "We are not in Rome my dear."

The Landsworth building does have a certain elegance, rising. The supporting piers are pillar-like, and the windows bend inward, slightly inset behind columns. Not far from us is the Widow Sloan, which disturbs me, a reminder of my ridiculous fainting spell. All of us, the closest to the speakers and the building itself, are horribly conspicuous in tail coats and brocade, as if a wandering tribe of misplaced nobles, rubbing closely with the city's actual vitality just yards away, those working the breweries, the river boats, and the land. There must be one hundred of them strangled together behind us.

"The beginning of a new era," Cartwright says, shouting over an increasingly violent wind. "It is a proud and soaring thing!"

"I was called that once," I say softly, this lost to the reckless wind.

*Soaring and statuesque.* That boy on the Mediterranean, my Augustine, that boy several years before Charles, that pale, poetic boy had said to me, "You are like a perfect statue, Dolores." I had laughed to hide my confusion. At sixteen I frightened most boys. I was tall with high cheek bones, wide eyes and an avalanche of hair. I was also told--that same year by an elderly woman with a face that could not hide a once startling beauty--that I was rare. She stood near me at a party, her ancient piqued face and throat set off by a mountain of velvet, fur and jewelry.

"You do not fool me. You know you are a great beauty and you are bright," she said. "But yours is a strong, not a delicate beauty. It is the type of beauty seldom seen since the Greeks' Hera. You are rare, my dear."

A woman's hat blows off, rescued quickly by her companion, and several carriages crawl around the corner. I am drifting, waiting here, ignored by Edna, focusing on the building itself. That old woman that called me rare is surely dust. And I no longer feel strong or rare. I will sneak my laudanum drops into a drink at the party. I will not tell Edna.

"Rising in sheer exaltation top to bottom without a single dissenting line," Cartwright continues.

I sigh, watching Cartwright, his failure to capture the crowd, these bricks rising but he, not rising rather lowering, like Augustine, he had fallen to one knee on a stone patio that overlooked the jeweled Mediterranean, and the angle of his wide knee had led me to notice, for the first time, in a sharp and threatening way, how horribly sad the beauty of the sea was, how immense and unapproachable. I had never had such thoughts.

"When will we escape?" Edna says, looping her arm in mine, dismissing the Widow Sloan who has been waving us over.

"He has got to finish soon."

There is an outdoor tent erected, and food on tables within the building, this for the working men and women. Despite the storm, the rising river, there will be fireworks and the drinking of beer. The river's threats, the levee's strain, seems to be discarded this evening to make way for loftier things.

Cartwright speaks of the structure's masculine strength. He is pointing to the top, a wide frieze and below that a deep cornice with decorated spandrels pierced by bull's eye windows letting in light. This startles me and I want to squeeze Edna's arm, to ask if she considers that strange, eyes looking into the very top of a structure as if it were looking into itself. And I think that is what memory is, really.

"Dolores, what is wrong? Are you going to faint again?" Edna says.

"I was only thinking of the past," I say, glancing away.

She touches my chin, commands my eyes. "It's going to be all right, Dolores," she says.

Finally, they cut the ribbon. Belasco Snopes says something. There is a smattering of applause.

"There is our carriage," Edna says.

Our group will not see the fireworks nor drink the beer. We will move on to the Landsworth estate to a private affair. Mr. Cartwright is coming toward us. I see Edna's back stiffen, her chin rise. I realize she is smitten with this swaggering man. He does not stop for Edna but rather comes to me, takes my gloved hand, and kisses it.

"I am surprised to see you. This is really out of hand," Cartwright says.

Edna gasps as the fine mist succumbs to a fast downpour. Mr. Cartwright throws his topcoat over our heads and ushers us speedily into a carriage.

There is a drastic bump as we get on our way. Mr. Cartwright smacks his cane on the roof and shouts at the driver. The rain rushes outside and Mr. Cartwright turns to face me. There is something ancient and indescribable in his look. Seeing Cartwright, I shiver with my recurring premonition that something terrible is about to happen.

# TWENTY-EIGHT

*A good paying job. Snopes' proposal. The shack.*

*Calhoun McBride*

He done whispered soft words dark and hot. There at the river, that night of our first coupling, then in his hotel room all those nights we met. I believed every word he said, held him close, together forever I dreamed, but that all went away fast, smashed to pieces, my bruised fist the only reminder of his touch. Guess there wasn't anything real to begin with as much as I wished there was. I'm riled, feeling beat up, angry and sad but I know the best thing to do is get away as fast as I can. I'm working the Landsworth party and making the last few dollars I need to take me West. I know I'll see Clement, which is risky since part of me wants one more look, one more touch and part of me wants to tear him to shreds. But I gotta keep my head on straight. Do the job, get the money, get on.

Landsworth himself was the first to talk to the help. He barked at everybody then we all got told what to do. My job is to walk around with a tray of champagne. It ain't crowded yet so my mind wanders. I know Clement will be here and I can't stop myself from thinking maybe he's gonna change his tune, maybe it's gonna go back to how it was. Maybe he's gonna yank me aside and say how he wants to get back to the river, or off somewhere we can be alone. But I know that's crazy. Looking toward the door it's like I conjured him up because in he comes, strolling with two ladies.

I stare straight at Clement but the only one who notices me is that Mrs. Brattridge. Her eyes spook me, the way they look long and hard. Clement sees me but he acts like I'm stone, like we never met and he laughs and smiles at the ladies which burns even worse and I feel a new and terrible hate rising in me, a deep knowing that this really is the end. I can't stand looking at him. They all turn away. My hands are shaking as I carry the tray. I gotta settle down. I conjure up a wide hot western plain, sky clear and water blue not muddy. That's where I'm headed.

I move into the next room and there's Mr. Belasco Snopes. He waves me over so I go offer him a drink. He don't take a drink, just lifts his hand, which is bird-like and white, and stays like that, staring at me.

"We meet again. The dirty little river drab," he says.

The room is starting to fill up and he don't budge, don't lift that skinny hand for a glass, don't say a thing, just looks straight into my eyes and I'm surprised he's talking to me, knowing what he knows about Clement and me. I wonder how much he knows, and what he might of said to Clement to make him toss me aside. I'm trying to recall what Bessie once told me about him. He squints real hard like he's about to pass a jail time sentence on me.

"Would you like a drink, sir?" I say.

"Absinthe and a sugar cube," he says real matter of fact. "Could you bring it to me in the back?"

He turns on his heel, fast, the way an actor might move on stage. He hurries toward the back of the room. I make my way to one of the three bars, get his drink, then head back. He's settled in a dark little corner smoking a long cigarette. His legs are folded over and he smiles as I get closer and his teeth look right puny and sawed off, but I think that's since his mouth is so small. He keeps on smiling, but somehow it looks like smiling hurts him. I stand in front of him, still balancing my tray. He takes the drink.

"You are an odd creature," he says, sucking long and hard on that cigarette, curling up his lips again like an actor shooting out the smoke in a long thin line.

It seems to me he considers himself to be something other than what most people see him to be. He holds the cigarette up, keeping that smile going, like it's stuck, like a crazy porcelain clown.

He displays two twenty-dollar bills, then folds them into his palm, all the while never losing that wide, awful smile. I never had that much money in my life. It would pay my train ticket and give me plenty to get started on a new life out West.

"How can I help you sir?"

"Come closer," he says. "I have a proposition for you."

Seems he knows the kinda work I do on the river. I'm pretty sure I know what's coming next and try to imagine what he might have in mind for his pleasure. I've found the richer the man, the darker the fantasy.

"I want to take you to a very special place," he says, eyes still shut.

"I'm working for Mr. Landsworth, sir."

His eyes snap open. "I'll pay, you dirty drab. I'll pay you forty dollars cash. But you have to go with me now."

I consider that. It's forty times what I'll make at the party. He begins to shake his head back and forth, then he pulls out a wad of money and presses it to his nose, sniffing.

"Money stinks of greed. I know you want it. You all want it. Shall I call my carriage?"

I see the money, and then I see the west wide open and empty, nothing but a long straight trail into some kind of endless, lonesome night. I curse Clement under my breath, then I set down the drink tray and let go of any last shreds of hope.

"All right," I say.

# TWENTY-NINE

Piglets. Bribes. A Tempest.

*Belasco Snopes*

*WILL HE CRAWL like a piglet? Snort snort little piggy. Or neigh like a horse biting the bit.*

The absinthe is wonderful. I will nick my ankle and inject cocaine once I'm out of this dreary crowd. Now I have the boy, he will bleed truths and vilify Cartwright. I will own that dreary architect. Will he resist, this one? That last one, oh dear, that Jenny Claire. Bloody mess. Filthy little thing. Thief. Dirty. All of them dirty. The drabs, the worker bees. The wet stink, the pawing and preening. They think they know things. They do not. I tear them open and then they understand, as best they can at their alley level. Deprived and delirious.

Making my way through the crowd I hear wild rushes of thunder above. Will my riverside hideaway sink? I do not see Landsworth. This will be an easy escape.

Ahead, near the front window, lingering in pearls and pink froth is that Edna, all gossip and soft wickedness. She guards Dolores Brattridge. The two of them, ridiculous school girls. Brattridge a vacuous prude. One hot wind would turn her to feather dust. She could so easily be taken, twisted, destroyed. But what's the point? She's already half dead. They are entwined with Cartwright and some Senator and the sight of them, hunkering there, all tails and sheen and high talk, sends a hot red flush to my face, a burning to my fingertips, a deep need to rip them apart. Cartwright sees me. He should bow to me and kiss my boots. Damn his empty bravado. But that soon will dissolve. He will be my slave.

My cigarette is nearly exhausted and I pause, drop it, squash it and there is an ashen Cartwright under my shoe, demolished and defrocked and I can breathe again.

I turn. The boy is following at a glacial pace. These river lads, skinny, lost, dim-eyed things, baptized by the river. Put to some good use before they fall back into their useless lives of drudgery.

"Cal...Houn," I say very softly, fixated on the cigarette butt now only black ash stranded on marble, obscene little gesture before I go.

Calhoun is ambling toward me. Will his skin bruise easily if he refuses to talk, to play my game, a lush lilac, a soft blood-lipped nipple shade? I shiver and laugh. Or he may just take the grubby money and spill his guts. He may need no coaxing. Edna sees me and turns, slashes those eyes open and shut, harlot really, though with that title, that wealth, she will always command respect.

Calhoun nears. The last one, no, two drabs ago. He begged me to save him from the rough trade, the gunk and strangling mud that lives on the shore. I had caught him stealing at the brewery and he did not run. I always wondered, why not run, you fool? I would not waste my time chasing you.

Instead he buckled, he squealed for me. Poor little piggy. Plucked, discarded. So easily.

This one, Calhoun, I pray, will fight and balk and offer some challenge to keep it exciting then he will tell me what I really need to know and he will sign it with his blood. I will discover Calhoun's full connection to Cartwright. There is the real prize: that idiot's final downfall. It will be a beautifully articulated destroying.

There is more rumbling from the storm, the throat of God opening to devour the lot of us. I've always known that St. Louis, in its muck and glory and absolute corruption, will be gobbled up, swallowed whole by a hungry river. Maybe today. And with me riding straight to hell on the back of a grubby little rocking horse.

Calhoun is very near, so I move swiftly, eyes down, head down, preacher-like, determined, a man of honor, out to my carriage. In front of the house, a torrent. Did I tell Bessie the tar bitch to stock my bar, to clean things up since last time? That one, Miss Bessie, that one is in cahoots with the devil for certain with her Southern spells and wicked tongue. Anything for a price, she says. Indeed. I believe I instructed her since last time with Jenny Claire.

I hurry to the carriage. Let the boy come to me drenched, soaked with the sweet salivating of a hungry God, the mouth torn open, bleeding muddy rain and hard bits of hail. He's standing at the Landsworth doorway, tied up in that tight little serving suit, gawking, lanky and dull, looking around. I wait, enjoying this. That mane of hair soaked, blowing snakes in the wind. I can barely contain my excitement. I shove a hand out the window, motion him over, and then get out my kit to inject my ankle at last. It is best to get to the river before the roads are impassable. Before the tempest eats us alive.

---

# THIRTY

*A river shack. Madman. Running.*

*Calhoun McBride*

SNOPES IS SLOSHING through a foot of water crossing cobblestones to a shack. If this rain keeps up it's a flood for sure. He's pushing through in his shiny brass button shoes, laughing, kicking at the slop, and I'm thinking maybe this ain't such a good idea. He cranes his neck back, rain soaking us both, river gunk floating to our ankles.

"Giddy up boy," he says.

Ever since we got out of the carriage and made our way past the Eads bridge, past some shanty folks, moving in the direction of Fat Frank's place, Snopes been turning into something else, talking loud to the thundering sky, shouting things back at me that make no sense. I seen this. Men that need to be something else at times. Before they get naked and ask to be called names. It don't matter. It's that laughing of his that spooks me. It's so fast and crazy. It ain't something I recollect hearing before. Still, that forty dollars is a fortune.

There's a fierce slash of lightning. Snopes' willowy arm points toward a shack up the hill. I seen it before but never been in it. It's painted black so it looks like there ain't no door but as we get closer I see brass hinges. Snopes fusses at the plank door then yanks it open with a thrust. A new gush of rain sets in and I'm happy to get under cover.

Inside the shack it's pitch black. Snopes laughs low and steady. I move a few steps forward into the darkness.

"Neigh for me," he says.

"I can't see nothing in the dark, sir. Is there a light?" I say

Snopes moves away, lights a lamp and I see a hard slash of blood across the floor and a big gold leaf mirror on the far wall and a fancy bar cart that looks like it belongs back at the Landsworth house. He's over at that bar fixing himself a drink. I ain't never seen a river place look so done up. I pause at the door, taking in that blood stain. My gut says turn around and go, but the forty dollars says keep your wits about you and get this done. He's a scrawny, sickly looking man. I don't figure him for dangerous, just flat out crazy. I'm sure I could knock him out if the need arises. I step further into the shack. His back is to me, and the black of his tail coat in the dim light just keeps up onto his black head as his shoulders rise.

"Neigh," he says. "Surrender to me the beast you are."

I consider this. I glance back at the door as a new rip of thunder hits. I want that forty dollars. I give it a try, making an animal kind of noise. He don't move, that black back, his black head, them soaked shined boots.

"Again, louder," he says.

I can tell there's some thrill in his voice so I figure I'm doing all right. I give it another try, then again, shutting my eyes, thinking of them fine beautiful animals. This time I go real loud and he starts to clap. His back is still to me.

"Good," he says, finally turning.

That's when I notice hanging on the side of that little bar is a cat o' nine tails. It's real skinny and slick leather with fine whip shards hanging down. I ain't fixing to get under that.

"I ain't gonna be whipped sir," I say. "You best tell me your pleasure."

He fiddles with his drink, looks over at the whip and smiles that wrecked clown smile.

"Oh no, no, of course not," he says. "That relic belonged to my father and his father before. Back before the war. We are no longer barbarians. Thanks to Mr. Lincoln."

"Can we do the payment first, if you don't mind?"

This startles him a little, but he keeps that crooked smile, takes out the bills and waves them like he's shaking a hanky off the bow of a ship.

"You get paid once I get what I desire," he says.

I hear the rain getting rougher, and water has begun to slip unwelcome under the shack door. I look at him. I can see the river is fixing to come into the room.

"Flooding comes fast sir, you sure you want to stay here?"

"Shut up. You shut up! I'm in charge here. And you are going to tell me what I need to know. I want you to write it down."

That surprises me. He ain't making sense.

"I don't understand," I say.

Water's running over the floor, through my feet. The thunder is making a good ruckus and the water is rushing faster. I seen a room fill up mighty quick when the river sets her mind to it. But I'm a good swimmer if it comes to that.

"What exactly were you doing in Clement Cartwright's hotel room?" he says.

It all the sudden dawns on me this ain't all what I thought it was. Is he trying to get me to write down what me and Clement did, to use it in some blackmail plot? The rain's thrashing harder and I think of that first time with Clement, the chances he took with a river rat like me, the way I felt like I never felt before and as much as I want to hate him, to see him hurt real bad, I know I can't. I know no matter what, I'll always hold close in my heart what he was to me.

"He was teaching me to read," I say.

"Liar!" he yells. "Get on your knees."

I move toward the door.

"Wait," he says. His face is a wild mask of terror and happiness. "Confess. Get on your knees and tell me the truth and I'll give you the money!"

Now he's coming my way.

"I got nothing to say against Mr. Cartwright," I say.

He considers this and it seems to calm him. He speaks softly and slowly. "Confess your own sins on your knees. Get on all fours and humble yourself like the lowly beast you are. Neigh for me. Do it and I will pay you. Then you can go. Please!"

He looks crazy but downright pitiful. I come this far, so I might as well finish. I get down and start into neighing. The water is rising a little. I'm waiting and look up to see where he is but he ain't nowhere. I see that whip ain't where it was and then he's behind me.

All the sudden he straddles my back likes he's riding me. Then he snaps that whip three hard times across my shoulders and he starts yelling and that catches me off balance. Then he hops off and kicks me hard.

"The beast will be undone," he screams. "Tell me what that devil Cartwright did. I want a written confession."

Before I can get up he's on top of me again, pressing my face hard into a puddle of water and I'm gagging and he's yelling some religious gunk and with a thrust I push him off and rise up and get to that bar. He runs to the lamp and puts it out. It's gone quiet, pitch black, just the sound of water coming in and then him.

"There is no turning back, I will break you, snap your back, and get you down into the water where we can redeem you. You can't save Cartwright."

I hear the sound of a gun cocking.

I grab what feels like a glass bottle off the bar and make for the door, blind. My foot hits something and that's when he's on me, smacking that whip, yelling again and I swing the bottle and it hits him and I hear him hit the floor with a thud. Another thunder crash and I'm running and when I fling open that door I see him there, face down in a pool of river water, and I don't care what happens to that mad one. There's a long terrible silence and I wonder if I done killed him. I step in and grab that forty dollars out of his pocket. Then I run as fast as I can.

PART THREE

# THIRTY-ONE

*Saviour. Daddy. A reckoning.*

*Belasco Snopes*

I LIFT MY moon-haloed head to see him go, his two-hoofed feet fleeing, that horned head and in his flight, I hear the answers. That dreary creature is my salvation. There is blood eking from my head and I am supine, flat in a warm and rushing pool of water here on the plank floor of my river shack, near the blood of those I've demolished, those I've saved, too, and as my purest blood flows, as it runs the river red I see how I will cleanse them all, and they will cower. Not just Clement, not just he, but this whole damned miserable city that has forsaken the Snopes name, the Snopes legacy, those who cackled secretly at Daddy's death, who would certainly not weep to see me drowned here by the likes of a dirty wretch named Calhoun.

I am dizzy, weak and cannot rise but I will rise, on the third day, the third hour, this third minute and I can hear him, Daddy, in the hot wind, so

I raise my head and there he is big and bold as Lucifer raging at me as he always did, wagging a fiery finger. *Get up son, get up. Don't snivel. Go out and conquer!*

And of course I will. It has all become so terribly clear.

# THIRTY-TWO

Escape. Fat Frank. Kin. Get the train.

*Calhoun McBride*

STORM SMASHES HARD at me like the fist of God. Lightning running wild and I think *"Go on slice me open, ain't nothing better coming my way. Ain't no turning back."*

Sloshing through a foot of water. The rain blurs my vision and I'm slipping on the cobblestones. It' the devil yanking me under, straight to hell. Running I think of turning back. Save the wretch if he ain't dead already. But my feet keep pushing through the weight of muddy flood waters and the fight to get West pushes me too, sweating in this jungle heat, thinking just a few more feet, get to Fat Frank's shack. Get to Fat Frank. Can't let it end like this.

Round the bend, river birch tree bowing so hard to break. The wind picks up and that tree snaps crashing down. There's Fat Frank's shack, a few more feet. I get to the door but it's locked so I start hollering and pounding, screaming over and over his name. Fat Frank opens the door, grizzled and fat, shirtless. He smiles at me and steps aside. His lips move but I can't hear him for the wind. He shuts the door, goes to the table and sits. He's been drinking a little.

"So, what you do now?" he says, pouring me out a snifter.

"Killed a man."

There weren't nothing else to say. There is quiet between us, wind howling outside, harsh breathy rumbles of thunder. The sound of constant rain.

"It's letting up a little," he says, drinking.

I drink, take in his girth and the way he sits, unflinching, like he's musing on a prayer, like things are smooth as Sunday.

"All right," he says. "Let's figure this out."

The battering rain quiets a bit, and I can't help shivering, this thing I done coming down on me, Snopes' face turned into drowning water. But Fat Frank is here with me, like kin, now and always. Far off, a train whistle hoots, and I lower my head, thinking how Fat Frank's like an idea slipping away. He won't be going West with me. It was three years ago I hopped off that Orphan train, and now I'm leaving again, leaving my only friend, my kin. Alone. Orphan all over.

I get up and go to him, put my arms around his neck and stay like that and he don't stiffen, he don't budge, he just lets it happen. I hang on, shaking in the heat. I want to crawl inside him, to hide in that old river warmth.

"Thank you," I say, letting go.

"You need to move fast," Fat Frank says. He pours another and sighs. "Anybody know yet?"

"Just happened. I ran."

"So, you best run now. Hop on the next train." Fat Frank gets up, takes a long look at me then goes back to his bed. I hear some rustling. He comes back with a fist of bills, lies them on the table. "This will get you started," he says.

"I got money," I say.

"I been saving this for you all along. Take it and hush."

I pick up the money. Put it in my pocket. "I'll pay you back every cent. Once I'm out west."

The door swings. It's Bessie. She slams the door, catches her breath.

"What did you do?" she screams. "What in the fuck were you thinking? You stupid little shit!"

She comes to the table and falls apart in a chair, letting her head droop and Fat Frank reaches out petting but she snaps that mighty black head up.

"That Snopes is running up the waterfront screaming how you tried to kill him. He's going to get the law. I was passing and he came right up to me and he slaps me hard across the face. 'You tell that dirty little river boy he's going to hang,' he says. That's just what he says. What did you do Calhoun?"

I think *"Well at least they can't get me for murder."* I touch that money in my pocket. Maybe I can hop a train and still run before they get to me.

"You ain't a murderer," Frank says, soft and quiet, gentle like he's taking my hand and stepping us both through a wide, cool doorway. "Get on, hurry."

# THIRTY-THREE

*Charles returns. Another dream. A scandal erupts.*

*Dolores Brattridge*

CHARLES IS RETURNING from Shanghai. The telegram lies on my dressing table, near a hair brush with ivory on its handle. He contracted a malady on the ship, they do not say which, and he is traveling back immediately with a nurse. He never set foot on the soil of what they call the Pearl of the Orient.

I am terribly troubled, not only by the news, but by the dream that woke me early this morning. I had the dream once before, the night I fainted at the Widow Sloan's. This time, beyond the rust-colored river rising, there is a boy naked on his belly on the cobblestone shore. In the dream, the boy is my lost son.

"Not uncommon sad to say," the Doctor had told Charles and I after the miscarriage. "There was an infection, scarring, these things happen. You will not be able to have children, I'm afraid. I know it sounds harsh, but I find it best if you don't dwell on it. Find a hobby."

He had taken Charles to the library and they had shut the door.

So, I started my garden, focusing my loss in the wet, black earth, that richness. Where had Charles buried his grief? I did not ask, just busied myself with my Rhododendrons and Hydrangea.

"How did you cope, Charles?" I say softly now.

We spoke of it only once, months later, in my garden. I was tending a parched bed of Azaleas. I looked up, blinded momentarily by a blazing summer sun and I saw Charles watching me, caught in a rush of grief, as if he were reclaiming a forgotten sadness. I reached up to him.

"I'm sorry Charles," I said. "I'm sorry I can't give you what you most want." He had not touched my outstretched hand, but instead bent down, his back to me, pinching the withered head off of an Azalea.

"It can't be helped," he muttered. Then he turned and left, not looking back. The next day he announced we would travel to Italy and France.

"St. Louis is too ungodly hot in the summer," he said.

I lift the ivory brush and stroke my hair. I cannot imagine Charles sick. His cheeks have always been rosy, his disposition hearty. I do not believe he will be ill when he returns, rather, that this will be some passing infection, some flush of illness that he will regard as the knotty bit which ruined his business trip. He will recuperate in my garden and we shall not speak again of the Orient.

The rain has finally stopped. A few shacks were flooded near the lip of the river. I overheard a servant say that a dog drowned.

There is a soft knock. It is my lady's maid. "Miss Edna is here, she says she must see you," she says.

"Send her up."

I take the telegram and hide it under my brush. It ought to be stained with my tears. I ought to be distraught. I lift it up again, and feign reading as Edna enters. Her dress is bold in multiple shades of red. She does not wear a hat and sits, out of breath, on my bed.

"Have heard the news?" she says.

She has not taken notice of the telegram. I set it down. "I heard from Charles," I say softly.

She is fussing with her hair. "Snopes is going to see that young man Calhoun hanged before end of day," she says, still breathless. "The claims he is making…it's a scandal."

I do not move. "Dolores?"

"Charles is ill."

She looks at me as if she did not hear, then tilts her head, glances at the flat, still telegram, my own fragile stillness, then she rushes to me. Her approach comes with a wild storm of memory unleashed, and Charles is young again and life is possible. I can hear his laughter.

"It's all right Dolores, I'm here." She holds me tight.

I begin to sob overwhelmed not with any one fear or reality, but with a terrible sense of loss, both past and present and, I now know the young man Snopes wants to hang is the boy in my dream, the boy I met in front of my house and I know, too, deeply, that Charles may be dying.

# THIRTY-FOUR

Rattlers in the desert. Dawn's coming. A voice.

*Calhoun McBride*

SOUND OF A rattler wakes me. Like stones shaking hard in a can. First slow then fast. I sit up and feel heat on my arm like the moon's gone afire. Get a glimpse of the snake, just a piece, slicing past me, and there's deep red on the tip of her, like blood passing through that hot moon onto that serpent's hide. She's a diamondback. I see the hard-angled shapes running down her body. Rattling stops. All goes quiet again and she's gone.

It's a clear night. Nothing ahead or behind me. Not a damn thing. Mile after mile. Night sounds. Coyotes, dogs, that rattler passing on, not bothering to fang my thick hide. I lay flat on a dirt bed. Sky stretching like a blackboard marked up with a million points of starlight. Nothing can erase all that. Nothing can get me here. Things crying out, searching one another.

Dawn soon. Ain't no use trying to sleep after hearing that old rattler.

Spooked me good.

Staring at this forever sky, shapeless as it appears, I wonder about cactus. Seems like it would be something to eat, the meat of that, after I yank the thorns. I heard if you crack into it, it spills its liquid like an opened skull. I know cactus lives a long time. Hundreds of years. Longer than me. That I'm damned sure of.

I sit up, dig a bit of rock out from the dirt, soften my lay down. Earlier I passed a tangle of smaller pale looking cactus, tiny orange flowers cutting out at spots. There was a whole mess of them twining together. Mangled and close like they was dancing to crazy desert music. Trying to remember where those cactus were. How far back. Land stretches so similar to itself, hard to figure out where I most recently been. Can't recall what day it is. Don't matter out here.

Lying back again sky seems brighter. Dawn's on the way. Far off there's a milky light and the cowing of them dogs. Thinking I hear water but that can't be. Gotta travel a while, further out. It seems far off in the horizon there is a shadow moving. I check the knife hid in my shoe.

In the desert a man can imagine things. That shadow far off, shapes itself. It is growing, turning and I see a hat. I sit up, squint. It is forming in the night, the milky light coming up so slowly beyond it, that shape black up against the far away whiteness. I stand up, check my shoe again. I can't recall the last face I saw, last voice I heard. The coyotes have gone quiet. The desert has gone dead still.

Figure is coming closer now, tall, and that hat. It ain't got no brim. I'm going to shout, but can't think what to yell. I try but can't yell. Nothing is clear to me. All the sudden I lose all sense, can't think of any one word or even how to move, but it is clear something is rattling again, but not the soft purr of the viper, not the blood red tip, but a harder sound, a deep lost rattling, coming from the throat of a dying desert, coming from something underneath me, not even that man, not him that's coming my way. This rattle goes harder and deeper and I cannot holler. I cannot.

Then I hear his voice.

"Calhoun."

He's standing outside my jail cell. Clement. He gives the bars another furious shake. "You were out cold. I thought they killed you."

Dry mouth, bones hurting. One deep cut on each cheek. I sit up and pain shoots through my right hand. That's the one they broke when they arrested me, caught me running toward the train. Almost made it. Almost. Ran so fast my shoes near broke in half. The sheriff 's man got me, threw me down. That was it.

"Need a piss," I say.

Groggy, at the cell's bucket. All that dry desert dreaming. Can't get my own spit up, can't get my tongue to work. I turn back to Clement, then sit on my cot. It was Clement in my dream, in that hat coming toward me.

"I'm going to get you a lawyer," he says.

He looks taller to me now. Through the bars, in a white suit. There's a flower in his button hole which I find peculiar. His eyes don't meet mine and I laugh, thinking how not so long ago we was fucking.

"Is it Friday?" I ask.

"Saturday. You have been unconscious. A doctor had a look at you. I'm finding you a lawyer." He speaks fast, in soft tones. His voice is familiar to me, but not the rest of him. Funny how being locked up can change the whole picture of things.

"Maybe you best stay out of it." He leans in and grabs the bars again and meets my eyes.

I'd like to feel his hands on the back of my head. I can't be much less than fond of him. I don't want him to have to see me swing. I'd like him to remember me how we was at the river. That way. I know—and I figure he must know—that there's no damn hope for me. Not when a man like Snopes is involved. Not when you're a speck of river dirt like me. I left the man for dead. That ain't gonna sit well with no judge or jury. "You might as well go," I say, then right away I regret it.

A jolt shoots up my back from deep in my heels to the top of my head and that desert dream dies out and my throat goes dry and tight and I see myself hanging in the public square and I think *This ones your only chance you fool!*

He shakes the bars again, like he's fixing to bust me out. Mrs. Turnblatt, the jailer's wife steps in with a steaming food tray. I realize I'm hungry.

"He needs food," she says. "He had a fever."

She's a large woman, heavy, with the big hands of a man, a hard face and a gentle way. She wears an apron and a key around her waist. She's got a fairly mighty bosom. I remember seeing her in my dreams, but then it weren't no dream. I remember her putting a cold rag on my head.

"Excuse me, sir." She gets into the cell and sets the tray on the floor by the bucket. It's a fine mess of food, better than I ate most of my life. "Take it slowly," she says to me in a maternal tone. "You been down a good spell." She smiles at me. "I told Henry he ought to put a bigger window in this cell," she says. "A man can't live without light. No matter what they say he done."

The jailer and his wife live in the front of the jailhouse. Cells in back. Courthouse is just around the corner. I'm the only prisoner at the moment.

"But then you are just a young one," she says, turning to go, then to Clement. "You are a kind man to come." She looks at him like he's a preacher off to help the damned, then lowers her head and speaks in a softer tone, "Ain't many would come see one that Mr. Snopes is hell-bent against."

"I'll be back with a lawyer," he says.

My head hurts bad. I watch Clement as he leaves, keeping my eyes on him until he's out of sight, comforted by the fact that he'll return.

# THIRTY-FIVE

*Poached eggs. Mr. Vest. A pity.*

*Belasco Snopes*

"I HAVE ALWAYS considered the poached egg a perfect dish. Eggs are creation, of course, yet in poaching, proper poaching that is, well you would be surprised Mr. Vest how the practice can be insanely difficult for the dim witted. Regardless, the perfect poached egg rests in that place of new creation, do you follow? It is life itself, and we ingest that."

At the other end of the table my lawyer Mr. Vest shifts in his chair listening and saying very little. He is a weathered, middle-aged man who could pass as a cattle rustler. I will elevate his level of discomfort as quickly as possible, gaining a swift upper hand, setting his teeth on edge by the time I finish demonizing not just the boy, but the architect, his lot, all of them. There will be slim traces of their blood in my wake. If only Mr. Vest weren't so dull.

"Mr. Snopes, or can I call you..."

"Mr. Snopes is fine."

"All right Mr. Snopes, if you could tell me again why you were there at the river?"

There is a scar on his neck, his whiskers are gray. He looks like a pile of nothing. But he has never lost a case in court. He is reportedly the finest attorney in the state.

"Will you write it down this time or will I be forced to repeat it over and over?"

Mr. Vest sighs, attempts to smile. "Just once more, I need to wrap my head around the whole thing."

His clumsy paws struggle to grasp the elegant china cup in front of him. The skin around Mr. Vest's meaty jaw is loose, but his eyes are wide and bold, studying me.

"This boy, Calhoun, he pleaded with me, told me his friend was in grave danger, was near death." I gently tap the egg.

"Why you?" Vest says. "Why would his sort ask you for help?"

He has finally lifted the tiny cup, which in his hands casts him as a creature in a fairy tale, the over-stuffed hare tampering with Alice's decanter. His cheeks I notice are very rosy, his eyebrows unwieldy.

"Do you expect me to understand the mind of a criminal?" I say.

"Please, go on."

"I was taken in. The level of his desperation struck me. I believe in redemption, that the lost can be found. I am too hopeful at times, I believe too strongly in people," I say, measuring his reaction, making sure this rehearsed bit sounds authentic.

He holds the miniature china cup to his fat lips.

"I pity the poor, I am disgusted by the corruption and how young men like McBride can be taken advantage of," I say. "I had a moment of..." I consider my phrasing, how to strike the right balance. "I was weak, moved by his plight. I knew the minute we entered that shack that I had been duped. But the boy was too quick for me. I did not put up a fight, I gave him my money but that was not his aim. He is of the type for whom violence is natural. He needed to rid himself of the evidence. So, he smashed my head and left me in a pool of my own blood to die."

At this point I touch the bandage on my head, the mending wound. I press it slightly so the blood begins anew. The white cloth goes scarlet.

"It is not just this boy we must triumph over…"

"No?" Vest lifts a hand. "What else do you have in mind?"

My head is throbbing and I hope more blood will seep as I bring this to a rousing conclusion. Mr. Vest must at least vaguely comprehend that the trial will create a scandal involving Cartwright. He must understand my larger goals. Mr. Vest has set down his cup and is watching me.

"Calhoun McBride is but one hapless victim in a vicious epidemic of vice and scandal, of young people thrust into that river, on that shore, driven to atrocity, to sell themselves and lose all human dignity, and it is you and I, yes us, we have let this happen. Our city is sinking in smut and degradation and no one has raised a hand to stop it. They raise a building, they fill their pockets, they come from Chicago to blare their horn, but none of us is giving heedance to the truth, the indisputable truth that our city is sinking in sin. No one is taking that in, Mr. Vest. So, it has fallen on me."

"I see," Vest says, emotionless.

He glances at his cup, up at me and I see in his face a level of disbelief and mild disgust. He is a simple type, the sort who cannot see the larger scheme of things. Pity.

I stab the yolk. Vest is still watching me.

"Eat your egg, Mr. Vest."

# THIRTY-SIX

*A noble visit. Horned cookies. Succumb.*

*Dolores Brattridge*

CHARLES IS IN and out of fever but no longer in grave danger. I have been told not to bother him.

"He must be left alone to rest. I know that's difficult for a woman," the Doctor says.

I wonder how he knows this, a woman's mind, what is difficult for her. I know he is married. I wonder what his wife thinks when he is gone or when she is alone. With Charles now an invalid, and I lady of the house, my mind has been my own, wandering, casting out in sometimes dark and dangerous directions. The house and servants have been brought back to full readiness, as if Charles may wake at any moment and demand a dinner party. The kitchen is bustling, the servants on alert. Claire, my ladies' maid, tells me all of this. She is the only one who knows the details of my days. I can trust her. She is no gossip.

"I will take the carriage today," I tell her.

"Alone?"

I do not answer. She knows not to ask twice. She can imagine that I am doing charity work, or fetching herbs the Doctor has requested, or visiting Edna. I do not tell her that I will call on Mr. Snopes and that I also hope to visit the poor young man in prison. I do not know if they allow a woman at the jail, but I know Mrs. Turnblatt and she is a sympathetic Christian.

In the carriage I think of what I may say to Mr. Snopes.

*"There was no crime. I know this as a fact. You must relent."*

He will call gnash his fangs and call me mad. He cannot know that when I was a girl, before my coming out and before my mind became cloudy, before Charles, I could tell my mother where to find lost items. I could tell my cousin to stop fibbing (the vase did not fall in the wind, you broke it) and I knew too often the unbridled truth about illness, how things would turn out. My mother told me it was instinct, not sorcery. She said to be cautious in what I share. My instincts ran deep as a river, she would say, but rivers are known for drownings. I knew as a girl that I would never bear a child, and that knowing was the only one I willfully set out to prove untrue. And, of course, that was a useless destroying.

With Snopes' outrageous telling, with the river receding and society whispering too often about the scandal, I know the accusations about the young man to be false. I also know that I will be part of some ultimate truth unfolding, no matter how ugly. Charles could temper this, could remove me, and could take us away. But Charles is ill and I had a dream of that boy, the same boy who stood on my lawn the night I stepped out in my satin slippers. I do not know what I will say to Mr. Snopes. It is never advisable to visit a single man alone. Yet, here I am, in the carriage, on my way.

It is a mild day after the terrible storm and oppressive heat. Mr. Snopes' home is in Lafayette Square, which is anomalous to his pomp, though there are rumors of the area's eventual decline as the more fashionable set moves west. His home, in particular the front lawn, is pristine. An elegant looking young man with white blond hair greets me and asks me to wait in the front sitting room. His demeanor is odd, though not off putting. I am grateful that he did no cause a scene, or question my arriving alone and without a calling card. The young man returns and asks if I would like coffee or tea. I decline both. He says Mr. Snopes will be down presently.

Far off is the tolling of bells. I do not recall which church is nearby, thought I know there is one, and that I have been inside of it. The bells are multiple, one lapping over another, the high then low ringing at once musical and chaotic. There is a large window open in the sitting room. The bells stop then begin anew, but with a melody. Their music is soothing and through the window comes a scent of lavender, which is part of Mr. Snopes's front garden. I am lulled, distracted from my stern errand, and think it may be best to create a fiction for my visit. I have a sudden, alarming vision of Charles waking, calling my name, sitting up in bed. The bells have stopped.

Mr. Snopes enters, and in that oily visage, the short and calculated steps, the false smile, the sharp and creased suit, the brilliant red flower in his button hole, it is in that that I regain my mission. The pale elegant valet follows him, a few steps behind, as if he were guarding a king. He is carrying a tray.

"You shock me, Mrs. Brattridge, shock me to my very core," Snopes holds in his right hand a small lace handkerchief, which he uses to tap his brow.

The valet deposits the silver tea setting, and then regains his place at the door. Snopes has not looked directly at me. He seems bothered by the heat. I take a seat near him.

"Tea?" he says, beginning to move fragile bone china the color of the sea.

"No, thank you," I say, deciding how to begin.

"To come unaccompanied, with violent criminals prowling our streets and riverfront, that disturbs me terribly, Mrs. Brattridge," Snopes says, stirring. "I know why you came, that is who you are. To see that I have survived the brutal attack, to offer your delicate words and soft support but this is no longer a delicate city. This attack is the blessing that has shaken me from my stupor, has set me to my true path."

There is a plate of horn-shaped cookies, sugar dusted. He snatches one. "Your dedication, to risk your own safety to see me, that only enflames the fire and passion of my mission, my singular vision of cleansing our city, of evicting the dealers in evil and decay. I am a rich man so I have the luxury of such a crusade."

Finally, he looks up at me.

"He is an innocent," I say.

His face does not move, nor his hand holding the horn shaped cookie. I see, however, a tiny fluttering movement in his eyes. Then the cookie is in his gobbling mouth.

"Bring us sherry," he says to the valet.

Under voluminous skirts, my legs tremble.

"How is your husband?" he says. "You do not look well. Which is understandable."

The valet has returned, replacing one silver tray with another. Mr. Snopes pours sherry and I take it, sip it, revived slightly by its heat. Mr. Snopes rises and goes to the window.

"I do not expect you to understand the work of men. The hard but necessary work."

He has his back to me and despite his finely tailored suit, there is a weak slope to his shoulders. Without that face, those black eyes staring at me, I can speak.

"He is an innocent, the boy. Is there no room for forgiveness, for redemption?" I say, imagining his reaction. "Perhaps you could save him."

There is a slight rise in those minor feminine shoulders. There is light through the window, but somehow, that light avoids him. He is of loose dark stuff, a hard bit of a man.

"I am not beyond approach," he says, softly. "I have done my penance. Still..." There is a sudden melody to his tone, a softer, gentler timber, but in that, too, something unseen and venomous. "Do you know the story of the Hyacinth?"

On a small table near the window three of those bold violet flowers are in a vase.

"There was a boy named Hyacinth who died throwing a discus, and the God Apollo turned the child into the Hyacinth flower to preserve his beauty," he says. "That was grace. Not so with Apollo's son Phaeton." He laughs gently, his back still to me.

I struggle to finish my sherry. I cannot stop trembling. My visit is not going well.

He turns to me abruptly. His face is flushed, eyes wide. His stare disarms me. "Apollo allowed his son his deepest wish, to drive his chariot, the chariot the god rode across the sky making the sun rise and set. Can you imagine such power? But his son, so haughty, he was greedy and selfish and evil and in doing as he wished, forcing his will, he rode higher, the horses frothed and careened, it was a spectacle!"

He is walking toward me. His fists are clenched, his look wild. "He died, of course. He wasted what could have been magnificent."

He comes to the side of my chair and places his hand on my shoulder.

"The mighty will fall, Mrs. Brattridge. Not just the boy, that one you wrongly call innocent. True, he is a pawn. Still he is a criminal. The others will face their destiny," he says. "Do you know much of Mr. Cartwright? Do you have any idea of what he is capable of?" He squeezes my shoulder.

I am frightened. "I must go," I say.

His hand remains. "We will crush the decadent. We will find strength together, Mrs. Brattridge. Can I count you as an ally?" His voice softens "I would not want to see you succumb to wickedness. I would not want to have to save you, too."

I stand up, releasing myself. "I have to get back to Charles."

He has swiftly moved back to his spot on the sofa, snatched another horn cookie. His tone elevates.

"Of course," he says brightly. "You are an absolute angel. Coming to offer support. And now you know our path. I am assured that I can count on you. But I expected nothing less."

I turn and flee, catching one blurred and terrible glimpse of him as I go, his visage suddenly lit from within, those feeble shoulders rising as if driven by black wings, his head lilting back to reveal a fiery and unimagined truth.

# THIRTY-SEVEN

*Calhoun in jail. You a preacher? A story of Indians.*

*Calhoun McBride*

"WHERE WAS YOU running?"

Twilight's come. Scant light makes its way through the bars on the window. I was studying that light, waiting for it to die out. Can't see who's out there past the cell door. Some old fool preacher I'd bet. Ain't no use getting off of this cot. Sure ain't gonna get on my knees to pray.

"Where was you running?" he says again.

"Don't matter," I say.

"Still, I'm asking."

The voice is creaky, like it belongs to somebody who's been talking way too long. I look back to the window, at the hard dusk shafts.

"You a preacher?" I ask.

"Lawyer."

"Oh, that's good news," I say. "I can't see ya."

"Stinks a bit up close," he says.

"Can't help that," I say.

"True," he says. "Smoke?" He comes to the bars. He looks worse for wear. Wide, grizzled fella. Wearing a full suit and vest but no hat, thick mess of gray hair swept back, wild bush of eyebrows and a craggy beard.

"You look more like a farmer," I say.

He chuckles.

"Well, I been traveling. My name's Finch."

He reaches a hand marked with cuts and dirt through the bars, offering a smoke. I take it, take the light, take him in.

"Where was you running to?" he says.

"Why you need to know?"

"I fix to prove you innocent. That's why."

"West," I say. "You think I got a chance?". "Every man's got a chance."

"You're an odd-looking fella," I say.

"Yeah?"

He steps out of the light, back into the hall and I hear him shuffle away. I ain't seen no one but the jailer and his wife, since Clement first came to see me promising a lawyer.

I hear voices from the front and I sit up. All the light in the cell is gone. Dusk is now night. I hate the darkness most in this cell.

The hall brightens. Old lawyer is back with a chair and a lamplight. He sits near the cell door on the hardback chair, a wide swath of light around him.

"Like I said, been traveling. My feet hurt," he says.

We sit in the still. I finish my smoke.

"I'd like to hear what happened," he says.

"What good's that? It's Snopes word against mine."

He reaches through the bars and I see he's got a flask. I take it.

"You think you're done for then?" he says.

I take a slug. Can't think what to say. Sitting in the dark, alone here, I been sinking pretty low. He reaches for the flask. We go back and forth that way.

"I been West myself," he says, drinking.

"He paying you?"

"Mr. Cartwright?" He nods.

He hands over the flask. "I was headed to California with my wife and little girl. Got a brother out there runs a tool business."

I move up closer, just to get a bit of that yellow light. Lean on the bar, listening to the old coot.

"Did all right until we got up in the Snake River Valley. This was when the Snake Indians was fighting a war with the white man. I shoulda turned back when we came upon the eyeless fella."

He lights up another smoke.

"What ya mean by that?" I say.

"Was a blazing hot day. Cutting across a dry patch trying to make some time before we stopped. First thought he was sleeping but came up close on him, lying there, naked and burnt alive, charred bones, his eye sockets plucked empty. Just blood sockets. Wife and girl were back in the wagon so I kept on, didn't want to get them riled. But I shoulda turned back then. Shoulda taken that warning and gone back East."

The lamplight blows a little with a night breeze and his figure moves in and out of darkness.

"You know the feeling, doing something you regret?" he says.

"I didn't do it like they are telling it," I say. "It was self-defense."

"I know. That's what Mr. Cartwright says. That's why I'm here."

"So you made it West?" I say.

He takes a long pause like he don't really want to remember. "Stopped that night. Made camp. I always figured it was all the night sounds, coyotes and such, made it so I never heard nothing. Hard to let that go. I didn't wake until the smoke got at me. We'd had a fire for supper so I ran out, thinking it hadn't gone all out. There was six of them, surrounding our wagon. They was standing just past a ring of fire circling us, six Injuns with faces painted like carnival folk, wearing all manner of white man clothes they must have stole off of their victims. Some just plain near naked. They was fixing to burn us up in our sleep. Never saw the point in that. If they wanted to rob us, no use in torching our things. The damnedest thing, my big mistake, was that I ran straight out at them."

The breeze is keeping him in and out of lamplight so I can't get a good look at his face.

"I woulda done the same I guess. Gone after them," I say.

"Ran straight out screaming and the first one sliced into my arm, then across my neck. Must of been aiming for my throat. Then he hit me hard in the head and I fell out for a time, woke up and the whole thing was afire. Blazing in the night."

"Oh hell," I say.

"The only thing they got was our horses. Killed my wife and child. Left me for dead."

The lamplight has settled down and I lean in, and I can see a scar scooting across the side of his neck.

"So you see I been in dire straits myself, son. And I made it out. I'm thinking you can, too."

I move back and lay on my cot.

"It's only thing that keeps me sane," he says. "I got a lot more to save before I'll ever be forgiven. It's my penance. Only thing keeps me going."

I hear him getting up, picking up his chair.

"I'll be back tomorrow with Mr. Cartwright. You can tell us the truth about what happened."

He's gone and I lie there in the dark, my eyes still lit thinking of that ring of fire, the hard and mean sounds of flames burning, charring flesh, eyeless men. At first, I can't sleep but for thinking of all that but then I remember the scar on the lawyer's cheek. The scar of a survivor. And at last I fade off, believing I might just have a chance. I might be worth saving after all.

# THIRTY-EIGHT

*The hunt. Edna's vanity. A fatal misstep.*

*Belasco Snopes*

MY FATHER REQUIRED that as a boy I shoot a gun, catch a fish, and be ready to set a knife's edge against the belly of the catch to discover the intricate beauty of what lies beneath. The trout's fragile spine, the deer's searing guts and soft inner chamber. The powerful thrust of a dislodged antler or the startling power of one dead eye, alone, staring up from a slicing board. Hunting is life, he said, and life requires precise action.

I have taken a center table at Biddemeyer's Tea Room. It is the best table in the place, a vanity spot, and will appeal to the Countess (or Edna, as she insists I call her). She will feel safe, free with her language, oblivious to my aim.

Preparation for the kill, my father said, is the most critical step. That moment when spear sinks into flesh—that is the last and simplest part of the killing. It is the set up and preparation that one must master.

Edna has arrived and is being escorted to my table, her hat a preposterous tower of violet, though her dress is simple and smart. A silver bucket of champagne sits on the table, and as she fusses and settles, the waiter pours. I lift my glass, as does she.

"To our fine city's redemption," I say.

She nods, sips but remains quiet. I intend to put her off step several times, appeal to her ego, and loosen her to a point of absolute uncertainty. She is not a stupid woman. I will need to be clever.

"I was delighted by your invitation. We have all been so worried after the attack. But we are only two?" she says. "You said Dolores was coming."

A bold lie on my part. "She is distraught with her husband's fever," I say. "And there is much I want to learn about you."

She smiles but I can see the confusion, the mild distrust.

"I knew I could count on you to help me," I say.

"With what?"

The waiter has set out oysters and shrimp.

"I hope you don't mind. I planned our luncheon," I say.

She sips her champagne and I can see in the layers of violet in her hat, a subtle webbing, and a spray of something white and floral, from the earth. "Tell me about the charity event," she says. "I was shocked to hear you could think of planning anything after all you've been through. And now they say there will be a trial. You must be distraught."

"If it were up to me the criminal would simply be..." I change course. "But that's not why I asked you here. In times of struggle, it helps me to help others."

I begin in earnest, having crafted a dazzling fiction involving orphans and despair. She is easily drawn in, her eyes narrowing at one dramatic exclamation (twins separated oh the grief!). By our third glass of champagne, and a plate of canapes, she is near the snare.

"We will bring in Mrs. Brattridge, she is such a giving soul," I say. "I was surprised when she threw that party for Mr. Cartwright."

"Surprised?" she says.

"She does so much already, why take on that?" I say. "You must know why? You two are like sisters."

The Countess holds her crystal flute aloft and through the yellowed champagne I see her blue eyes as if jaundiced by the liquor, as they widen in wonder, opening to that childish place where women begin to trust a stranger, to soften, unknown. The jaws of metal are poised.

"Oh well, he is a bit of a celebrity in his own right, and dashing," she says. "Who can help but be smitten? And he was so kind to take her home the day she fainted at the Widow Sloan's." She sets down her glass and the bare touch of crystal is for me that delicate snap of the vice on her neck.

"Smitten?" I say. "A married woman smitten with an artist bachelor? A man whose reputation is not only sullied but of late absolutely in question by his association with my attacker. I had no idea she had developed a relationship with him. You do know he advocates for that young cad. He has found him a lawyer."

There is a gentle pause as my words fully land. Remaining still, her hands tremble slightly and I know it as the pain and mild panic of the captured.

"I've chosen the wrong words" she says. "I can only speak for myself."

"I'm afraid you have revealed the right words," I say. "You see the trail of depravity, you understand that the true evil in all of this is not that boy, it leads straight to Mr. Cartwright. I think you have always known that. And I am here to make sure none of this gets too close to our dear, Mrs. Brattridge.

For I am afraid for her, deeply afraid she may be ruined by association. He has surely already wielded power over her."

Her face is flushed, her eyes wide, like the eyes of the strangled, like that one wide shivering black eye of the deer as the socket is flooded gently with an unseen vessel of blood, as the black angel comes close. I have seen that look so many times and it never ceases to thrill. I hold the moment for as long as possible. Then I continue.

"I am afraid she may have gone too far already. But we can help her. You need to tell me everything you know about Mr. Cartwright. Leave nothing out," I say. "That's the only way we can make sure Mrs. Brattridge remains innocent. Who knows what will happen at the trial."

They have brought a poached albino pear and her skin has lost all color, as if she has been dragged from a place of living to that of the dead. Her eyes are aflame with calculation and I can see I have her exactly where I want her.

"Take your time," I say.

She does, the words tumbling. It is with these words that my plot so easily begins to take its perfect shape.

# THIRTY-NINE

*Fine visitors. A fly in the works. Tell the story.*

*Calhoun McBride*

THEY LET THEM both in my cell. Even brought chairs. Clement and Finch. We're not saying nothing. There's a shard of sun creeps in this time of morning. A swarm of flies that lately found me, cutting through that bit of sunlight. The sound of them buzzing gives me queer comfort. Like they're singing to me. Took them a while to find me, them flies. The stink must of drew them. I don't like how they light on my bandages, tangling in dried blood. Makes me itch. But their tiny cries are better than the dead silence. A cell is a mighty lonely place. These two men been staring at me awhile.

"We need to work fast," Clement says.

"You don't look good," I say.

This makes the old lawyer chuckle. Truth is Clement looks beat, his face pale and his eyes sunken. Like he's been crying or facing something he just can't stand to face. Like death. I quit swatting the flies some time ago and am used to them on me, but they really bother the gentlemen. They wave at them most constantly. Clement stands up and goes to the cell door, grabbing it, and there's that wide arch of his back, that hard beauty. I touched and kissed that back. He turns to me.

"I don't want him messed up in this," I say to Finch.

Clement comes toward me, sinks his hands into my forearms, and yanks me up off the cot. He near lifts me up and off the floor, pulling me so close I can smell licorice which must be his soap, and smell whiskey and see a horror in his eyes. He's strong and holds me near aloft. The grizzled old lawyer stands up.

"Snopes is doing this out of spite," Clement says. "We need to fight this together. I won't let him get you."

"Mr. Cartwright," the lawyer says.

Clement keeps holding me tight like that, leaving a mark on my arms, squeezing hard, and I feel the other part of his holding and I know he misses that, too, and he keeps me there despite my stink and the bruised-up look of me. It's all I can do not to lean in close and whisper something stupid but true. Finally, he drops me back on the cot. The lawyer clears his throat and sits back down.

"I reckon we best hear his story, Mr. Cartwright. This is doing us no good," he says. "We need to build our cast."

Cartwright takes his seat next to the lawyer and they both look at me.

"Tell it straight," the lawyer says.

"Got a smoke?" I say.

Clement lights one and hands it over.

"We was at the party," I say.

The lawyer takes out a paper and pencil.

"What you doing with that?"

"I'm old. If I don't write things down I won't likely remember and you'd have to tell it all again," he says.

I consider that, and get on with it.

"I was working at the Landsworth party. I got Mr. Snopes a drank and he asked me to leave with him. He said he'd pay me forty dollars. He showed me the money."

"What was he paying you for exactly?" Finch asks. "Speak plainly, son."

Clement looks up and I don't want to see them eyes. I figured, since they caught me, that this all happened because I invited in some of Snopes' evil. I'd always heard of a wrathful God. I'm starting to believe in that.

"I figured he was paying for sex."

I didn't expect Finch to whistle. "That's a lot of money for sex."

"He's rich and crazy. I figured he had some special thing he liked."

Clement clasps his hands together and I wonder if he's praying. I wonder if things had gone different, if he mighta gone away with me. I can't seem to get rid of that crazy dream of mine.

"He gets me off to the river, to this shack. That's when things changed."

There's one particular fly won't leave me be. Seems hell bent on settling into a wound on my arm. I start swatting it every few words.

"Inside that shack, I knew things weren't right. He had a wild look and he kept asking me about Clement. He wanted me to confess something and write it down. I decided he was plain crazy. You sure you want to hear all of this?"

"Go on," Finch says.

"He told me to get on my knees and neigh like a horse. He got a whip and started using it on me but I pushed him off. Then he blew out the light. It got pitch black and I heard him cocking the gun. I got a bottle and hit him over the head with it. And I left him there."

Finch lets out a heavy sigh and a light belch. "That's it?"

"Yeah," I say. "And I took the forty dollars. You know that part. And I left him to die."

"We'll need to leave out that part about you leaving him to die," Finch says. "I'm going to do everything I can to keep you off the stand. Snopes has a very different story. But if it comes to that, focus on the gun. It was self-defense. He was fixing to shoot you so you hit him over the head with the bottle. You taking the money can't be helped."

Clement is staring at me like he sees the blackness running through my sorry veins. I think I might just pass out. My head feels so hot and empty.

"Well I'll admit this ain't gonna be easy," says the lawyer. "But don't lose faith, son. We both believe in you.".

Clement is still, hands prayer clenched. I feel a soreness in my gut that makes me want to crawl into the darkest dark. But I don't 'cause I see now they really do have hope for me and I figure the least I can do is have some hope too. Maybe that's my penance. That stranded hope.

# FORTY

*A trip to jail. Mrs. Turnblatt. Washing Calhoun's wounds.*

*Dolores Brattridge*

FROM THE OUTSIDE it is not an especially imposing building. Square and brick, worn by the elements. On high ground to avoid the river's wet and deadly kiss. I have made it this far, practiced my speech for the jailer's wife, the kind Mrs. Turnblatt. Yet I cannot move. The magnitude of my action overwhelms me. I cannot shake my fear of the vile Mr. Snopes.

Yesterday, when I first thought of visiting Calhoun in jail, I had spoken in whispers to Charles, though his eyes only fluttered once, his hair wet with a returning fever, that bothersome nurse hovering. I sent her for tea, and sat close at his bedside, placing my hand on his forehead as if soothing a child. I brought my lips to his ear, and gently told him my plan.

"Charles, I need to save the young man named Calhoun. He is an innocent soul. I am sure of it."

With my touch, his breathing became more even.

"He is like our lost child, Charles, like all of my wasted hours, he is more then he appears and I am going to fight for him," I said, lying my face on his, making no effort to stop the tears. "I've done so little in my life. Nothing of true consequence. This is my chance."

When the nurse returned, she accepted my grieving. She stood, arms folded military fashion and waited, glowering at me, the weakness of rich, pampered women, she must have thought, the frailty.

But now, at the jail stairs, I falter. The front door swings and it is Mr. Cartwright. He is moving quickly with a disheveled older man. He stops, noticing me, caught there, and holding my eyes as he has done each time we have met always in odd circumstances, in destined ways.

"Mrs. Brattridge," he says, taking my hands.

"I've come to see what I could do for the young man," I say.

He is holding my hands still, in a way too intimate for the steps of a jail. He glances back toward the doorway.

"Speak to him," he says, softly. "He needs all of our help. Convince him there is hope."

With that he turns and leaves, followed by the ragged man, but as he releases my hands it is as if he has propelled me toward the stairs, into the jail. It is dim. Mrs. Turnblatt is there, sewing. She does not seem startled by my presence.

"Well bless you," she says. "Have you come to see him? The lost one?"

"Yes, I have."

She ushers me in without fanfare and I am no longer afraid. He is kept in back. Mrs. Turnblatt places a chair at the cell door. "Bless you," she says again, before leaving.

He is asleep, stretched across a tattered cot the color of straw. There is an animal smell, an earthy scent of country, this mixing with the dank odor of a tomb. I don't recall him being so lanky. He is dressed in rags, his black hair a tangled mess reaching high as if ratted into a crown. I remembered him as common but now, stretched there, arms over his head, long legs spilling over the edge, he appears elegant, and somehow beautiful to me. There are lavender bruises on his arms and legs and one gash that does not appear to be healing. Constantly, there is a buzzing of flies. I rise and go to find Mrs. Turnblatt.

"Do you have a cloth and a dish of water?" I ask.

She has come out of a small kitchen area leading to the space she and her husband call a home.

"He needs his wounds cleaned. They look infected," I say.

"The doctor saw him, Ma'am," she says. "I can't let you in his cell."

I know I am going too far. Still. "I understand. But he needs attending to," I say.

She begins to speak, then smiles, the defeated smile of an underling, someone who is certain they know better, but who does not have the rank to speak their truth. This, I realize, is likely to spur gossip. This may not be considered a blessed act. She steps out, and then returns with a small basin and a white rag. Her eyes do not meet mine. I take it and go back to the cell door. She does not follow.

He has not stirred. All is quiet save for the melody of the insects and it is in that droning melody, that derelict but constant tone that I understand my role. A mission that will ruin me. But a mission I was always meant to do. My mind is very clear.

"I am part of your saving," I say.

Mrs. Turnblatt is behind me. "I'll be serving his supper now." She moves to the bars, rattling them, and the boy stirs. He twists his body and sits up, staring out.

I am still holding the basin. "I am a friend of Mr. Cartwright."

"I know who you are, Ma'am." He wraps his arms around himself, as if he were caught naked. There are rips in his shirt.

"I have warm water for that cut on your arm," I say.

He lifts his arm, swats at the flies.

"Why don't you take this, put the rag over the wound," I say.

Slowly, he rises, stretching broadly, not the expected movements of a caged prisoner. He reaches through the bars and instead of handing him the basin, I gently place the warm cloth on the suspect wound. He lets me do this, sighing and placing his head against the bars, his face now closer.

"Your eyes are pretty," he says. "I never seen eyes that color."

"They are blue but can appear violet. It's the light."

Mrs. Turnblatt has returned with a tray.

"I'll need to get in there, Ma'am."

I step aside, leaving him with the rag on his arm. She does her work, and I step further back.

He tilts his head way back and the soup spills down his chin. I am struck with an image of him in the desert, a washwhite light and a brilliant sky that I know will someday be his. I turn and go. I do not look back at him, nor do I stop to wish Mrs. Turnblatt a good day.

# FORTY-ONE

*Two monkeys. He has never lost a case.*

*Belasco Snopes*

MR. TWOMBLY AND Mr. Vest sit side by side, two wind-up monkeys, the porcelain type with paws clutching tambourines, each mouth a cheap slash of red. They are trying to convince me that a trial is unnecessary. It can be settled out of court. Avoid any scandal.

"I went to a great deal of trouble to make sure you prosecuted this case Mr. Vest." In truth it was not difficult, just expensive, to convince the local prosecuting attorney to do things my way, to allow me to have my own council. "You do not seem to understand my goals."

The imbeciles must be made to understand the intricacy of my plan, the genius of it. The destruction of Cartwright. It will be an immaculately staged show, a hanging, but not the young man, no, it will be Cartwright whose neck will snap, whose eyes will bulge and run with blood. It all needs to happen on a large public stage.

I am propped in my four-poster bed and they have taken two narrow wooden chairs with legs as thin as a spider's. Their discomfort is clear. One wrong move and the chair legs could snap.

"We can't ignore that he's telling a different story," says Vest. "He says you asked him there, you wanted him to confess something. And there's the fact that you own that shack."

"My family owns most of this city. I can't be bothered to know every detail. That is Twombly's job."

"But you had been to the shack before. Some of your personal items were found there after the incident. In your story you said he led you there."

My skin bristles.

"My story! It is not my story it is the truth. That river trash has access to the shack. Perhaps he stole my things when he was working at the brewery. He is the criminal here. Do I have to tell you how to run this case? Get your head on straight, sir."

I would like to step away for a cocaine injection but I will not give the ape the satisfaction. I must keep my composure. I will speak privately with Twombly. He will need to do a clean sweep and destroy any scant evidence of my past transgressions to be safe. Discard any trace of that naughty little Jenny Claire. Luckily, I saved a lock of her hair, hidden right here under the pillow behind my back. Dare I pull it out and put it in my mouth while they watch? I smile at Mr. Vest.

"Remember Sir, Calhoun McBride is a liar, a prostitute, and a thief. What does it matter what he says? I am a Snopes."

Mr. Vest shifts in the narrow chair and I see the spindly legs teeter. He stands.

"There is the issue of Belinda's wedding," Twombly begins, all nerves and edge. "Even if we win."

"If?" I shout.

"When we win, of course, it's a clear-cut case. But why drag yourself through all of this? I think he will confess to assault if we offer a deal." Twombly says. "We can get him put away and leave this behind us."

"I want this city to know what I went through, and how deeply depravity runs amuck. I want them to see the offspring of their plans, their insistence at bringing in a Chicago man to do a St. Louis job, how that is what laid the groundwork for a crime like this," I say. "I want him to suffer."

"You want McBride to suffer. Yes, I see that," says Vest.

These two have been pecking at me for some time. I try another tack. "You are missing the opportunity here to benefit your own career, Mr. Vest," I begin. "This will elevate the Snopes name and your affiliation with me. We will reveal our true purpose! We will get at the source of what infests our city. This can be the beginning of a farrowing out. I see bigger things for you, Mr. Vest."

"And what of Belinda?" Twombly says. "We could send her away."

I have tired of them both. This interview is done. "She will be at my side, the bright flower that she is. She will show our family's softer side," I say, in my mind these two gone, my evening's pleasure already beginning. "There's nothing more to say. See the Judge. Spread some money around. Get this on a fast track."

Vest, scratching his flabby chin, has turned to study a Spanish painter's depiction of a panther devouring a peasant.

"It's wonderful isn't it," I say. "The beautiful, the powerful gobbling up the weak, the useless."

Vest does not look away, hand still on that awful chin. "I don't follow."

"The panther, sleek and elegant, is a rabid carnivore. He only eats meat, mostly the feral hog, the white tail deer and on occasion, an alligator," I say. "He is also a strong climber and can shimmy up a tree, ambushing his prey from above."

"Interesting," Vest says looking over at me.

I know, in that brief moment, that he considers me propped in bed, covered in mink, not only eccentric but perhaps insane. I would like to throw him into the oil painting, to shove his fat head into the drooling jaws of the panther, to be rid of the honorable Mr. Vest. But he has never lost a case.

"I have been atop that building, Cartwright's skyscraper, and like the panther I have looked down on my prey and seen his rotting insides. I have seen that," I say. "I will put that man in his place."

Twombly begins to gather his papers." Mr. Snopes has always had the poet's mind," he says rapidly. "We have all we need. I will see you out Mr. Vest."

# FORTY-TWO

*A hysterical bar. The plan. Two visitors out front.*

*Clement Cartwright*

"THIS AIN'T GONNA be simple no matter what angle we take."

I'm meeting with Finch, Calhoun's lawyer. We've hunkered into a corner table in the Taj lounge at the Planter's House Hotel. It's a chaotic room, overdone and hysterical. I'd like to rip it apart, strip the fake gold off the walls, and set the silk cushions on fire. It's a fatal mishap in an otherwise beautifully designed hotel.

"Do you believe him?" I say.

Finch, who looks unwashed and sweaty in ancient tweeds, rubs his grizzled chin and shakes his head. "Let's get another whiskey," he says, waving for a drink.

An olive-skinned waiter in an outfit as crazed as the room, all blue silk and Indian jodhpurs, brings over a round. "It ain't whether I believe him, it's what the jury will think," he says. "It's whether his version of the story is believable."

"But do you?" I say, not hiding my irritation.

Finch takes up the new drink and sniffs it. "This is good stuff. I'd say he's likely telling the truth. He doesn't seem to have the smarts to be cooking up a scheme. My problem is this. I can't fathom why Snopes is going through all this trouble to get at you and bring you down, which is your explanation. Especially if there's any truth in what Calhoun says. Why put his family name through the wringer? All because of that Wainwright deal?"

"He's spiteful. He's using Calhoun," I say. "He thinks he can ruin me. And he wants to put on a show."

"In what way?" Finch downs his whiskey. "What could that kid know about you and who cares two hoots. I'm a sensible man and none of this makes any sense."

I stay silent. He takes that in and there's a slow gentle softening to the mess of hard lines of living on his face. He is considering me more closely.

"Is there anything I need to know?" Finch says.

I lift my whiskey.

"I don't want to see a young man wrongly accused," I say. "I feel responsible. And I'm fond of him. I'm the one Snopes is really after."

He nods, rubs his chin again. I can see he is not convinced and I also see a dawning, that recognition that is cast aside, too awful for his sort to comprehend.

"I'm gonna need a place to stay and some money for the essentials if I'm gonna give this a good run," he says.

"I'll get you a room here. We'll settle that up," I say.

The waiter has returned and stands near me. "I'm sorry, Mr. Cartwright." His voice is gentle, as soft and feline as the silk he wears.

"There is someone asking for you."

"Yes?"

"They are outside the hotel."

"Well bring them in, what's this about?" I say.

"That's impossible."

The young man's face is flushed. "If you can follow me." The waiter turns in a flurry of blue.

"Well ain't that something," Finch says.

I get up and follow. Outside the Planter's House Hotel, I first see no one. Turning to go, I spot the pair across the street. He's a very large black man wearing a bright, almost comical looking suit coat and mismatched pants. She is tall, thin, tar skinned, wearing a lot of lace and a hat with a purple plume that lacks any discipline or art. They look like curious circus folk. The man raises his hand and I cross the street. They cower as I near, bowing their heads as if I were some deity. He gets right to it, in a voice rich, dark and steady.

"We here for Calhoun. He didn't do it. I want to testify."

I never learned where Calhoun lived, nor asked about his family. "I know he's innocent," I say.

"How you aim to save him," the man says, then from her, "Or do you?" Her voice is high pitched with a ragged quality.

"I've hired a lawyer. We're working up our case. Self-defense."

In the still, there is a train whistle. I wonder how long until the railway suffocates the riverboats, sheds its long smoky shadow over the river that this city loves so well.

"We know things," she says, again in that high pitch histrionic. "About Snopes. I know things he done. Terrible things."

At that she steps back, as if her own words could snap back and burn her skin, or snake in through her taut, blood painted lips, down her throat to strangle her.

"You need to know," she says softly, stepping back again and then bowing her head. "Oh lord. Oh lord, protect me."

The big black man comforts her, embracing her as she cries and for the moment they seem to have forgotten me. The train shrieks again in the distance and she gasps, then they both look at me.

"You gotta save him. You gotta help," the man says.

"All right. Tell me what you know."

# FORTY-THREE

*A dream of Charles.*

*Dolores Brattridge*

CHARLES IS DEAD.

No one knows this yet. His cheeks are rose-flushed and he is warm, hands folded over the top of the bed sheet, his hair neatly brushed across his beautiful forehead.

I am lying at his side and have been awake for some time.

"Come inside now, Dolores," he said to me, speaking so clearly in my dream, wearing his favorite summer suit, on the lawn, somehow younger than he was when I first met him, checking his pocket watch then calling me again as if I were the errant girl he married, as if he were fearful of a coming storm. "It's time dear."

I had woken and turned to him, knowing with a calm certainty that he was gone.

It is now barely dawn, that time when the light is so very dream-like, so striking. My vision of a mist, a gentle ghost taking shape and moving across the bedroom does not frighten me. I relish it, for it is the very last of him, the timbre of his remembered voice, and the tread of his bare feet on the carpet. I have placed my hand on his arm and am speaking to him in a hushed voice.

"I failed you, Charles," I begin. "The son we never had. But I am going to make that right."

I have always believed in spirits, in souls lingering. There are things I must say to him quickly before the nurse barges in. Things I would never dare say, things I often wished to say. There will be ample time for grief. I must speak before his spirit flees. I do not know the exact ways of spirits, but I imagine this moment, this brief half-time between life and death, is when he remains most close to me.

"Do not scold me Charles," I grip his arm and for a moment I imagine he will turn his face to mine, will smile, will ask for a last kiss. "I will save that young man, that lost soul in jail. He is good. I know he is good. I have always known things, Charles. Just as I know you loved me."

The window is wide open, and the curtains rise with an angry wind. There is in the light a formed spirit that scolds me. He does not understand. He never accepted my ability to "see" things. That was not Charles in life. It is not Charles in death.

"I will not disgrace you, I promise," I say quietly, shutting my eyes, burying my face in the scent of him, in his chest. "You may haunt me dear. You were always so good to me. I will make you proud of me. Wait and see."

There is a commotion in the hall. That bull of a nurse is ordering my maid about. A soft knock. I do not answer. I remain quiet but I know that they will soon enter. The nurse will come in, will check his pulse, my maid will arrive with coffee. The window curtain has settled; the spirit gone. His arm is cold now. I want to pry open his eyes, to find a final tear there, to make him see me as I truly am, as I am at this very moment. I want to speak to him.

My hand touches those pale eyelids but then there it is. The door creaks, the nurse with her own sense of knowing hurries over, presses my hand away, probing. My maid, too, is there with the silver tray and she waits, pale. Death is that way. It announces itself. I remove myself from the scene, I go to bathe, I prepare to grieve properly but glance back once at him, dreaming that he may have opened his eyes, or return to the lawn where I saw him before waking, him with pocket watch, him scolding me, him loving me in that way that no other man ever will again, or ever could.

"I love you Charles," I whisper. Then I go.

# FORTY-FOUR

*A night swim. The drabs.*

*Belasco Snopes*

WHAT DID DADDY always say of swimming in the river? It is good for the drabs, the commoners. They can share with one another their disease of being lowly slithering through the muddy Mississippi. They can soak their feeble minds and tarnished bodies. "You must never allow that water to touch your skin," he said. "We are chaste. It will destroy you."

And what would he say now? I here at river's edge, far off from the steamboats, from my own beer wagons and workers, my clothing in a neat pile, my pale nakedness an offense to no one. But then Daddy is dead and I am here, on the brink of my greatest triumph.

I hesitate, before my feet touch the water and shudder with an ancient fear, his fear. If the drabs come too close it is like acid on gold. It can stain and diminish even the purest and strongest.

I step forward. The warm muddy water seeps into my toes. I shiver with a new knowing, my own knowing— not at all Daddy's. I have transcended all he imagined. I am untouchable.

I linger at river's edge, thinking how simple it is to spill the seed of doubt into the minds of ordinary men. They may try to hush me, but they will never look at Cartwright again without a trace of doubt once I am through with him. I have infested the crop. I have begun my slow whittling down. My attack on Cartwright is underway.

I step in up to my knees. The water is warm, like the womb, and the rocky ground slides to mud then to nothing. My waist sinks, my arms slop through the water and I go further. I do not hesitate as my head submerges with dirty baptism. Let the putrid water touch my lips, enter my mouth, lash my tongue. I even open my eyes underwater and see the blackness in the river, the debris and gunk. I come up for breath and float on my back. I am filthy now, but it matters not. I have rebuked and can rebuke any attempt to damn me, to outwit me, to yank me under. I have stepped into their primordial ooze and I have beaten it. I did not grow weak or sickly with its touch, as Daddy predicted. I am thriving. He is dead and I am here. I am floating gently.

I submerge again and stay under in muddy blackness, ready for the dawn.

# PART FOUR

# THE TRIAL

# FORTY-FIVE

*To court. That funny bird.*

THEY DRAG ME out stinking and ugly past the gawkers in front of the jail, yanking me past men cussing hard threats and I think this must be what our lord savior felt like being taken to slaughter.

I'm shaggy and rough, though the jailer lady gave me a swipe of a comb and a pat on the head like I was off to school. My eyes burn, since I been in that black cell, and now am shucked into the daylight. The policeman Mr. Granger pulls me up a cobblestone walk, round to the stairs of the mighty courthouse. The stairway is crowded with more gawkers pointing and spitting but I look east and see her, hear her, the river charging on and I think I'm gonna get away, gonna dive in and get away somehow. At the bottom of the steps Granger stops.

"You all right?" he says softly, which surprises me.

"Yes, sir."

We start up and I recognize a lot of them, eyes wide and white-flamed, mouths wide and foaming like they want to tear into me, chew me up, and spit the pieces into the Snopes' brewery smokestack. We're climbing the wide stone stairs past the yowling lot of men. Skinny Merle the barber with one bad eye, the red headed Carlton boys I played poker with not long ago, and Danny Boyle who slapped me on the back telling one of his longwinded jokes just last month. And back behind them, wearing something bright and silky is that crazy Pretty Boy Pete, biggest river poof I know. He ain't been seen out in daylight for years. They're cussing, like I ain't the person I was, like I got turned into a demon. Granger takes me up to those big double front doors and shoves me inside, then twists back with a shout to the crowd.

"The judge ain't gonna put up with no malarkey, boys, so Merle you best leave your flask in your pocket. This is gonna be a civilized trial, not a hog spectacle. I'll be seeing to that."

The courthouse hallway is cool and quiet like a church. The floor is cold marble and the walls are dark. Granger takes me down the hall and straight into the court room. First time I ever seen it and it's grand with long wood pews crammed with people, a throne like thing up front for the judge, and a balcony for the Negroes. Above it all is a giant half circle dome letting the sky in. They all turn and look hard at me like I've already lost. And I wonder if it will matter two shits that I'm innocent. Will the dirty likes of me have a chance? Like he heard my thoughts, a man sitting up front turns, hunched shoulders, oily shock of black hair and a bright blood red flower in his button hole. Belasco Snopes. He bears his ugly fangs with the scariest smile I ever seen.

Granger takes me on while the crowd whispers. He sets me next to my lawyer, Mr. Finch, across from Snopes' lawyer, Mr. Vest. There must be fifty people filling the long pews behind me and we're all under the dome and it feels like all the light's coming on me, so bright it hurts and frightens me, like God opened one wide angry eye to stare down with finger-pointing damnation. Even God figures I must be guilty. Then I see the dove. It's skirting around, bashing up there in the dome and two starched up old ladies in the audience (the snooty Polk sisters who look so much alike nobody knows which is which) look up and cross themselves, watching the bird circle the giant dome, cutting into the sunlight, moving around the lower part, then going higher like it could bust through the top. All the sudden I think I gotta get free. I can't rot in jail. I gotta get outta here.

The judge enters from a side door and climbs up into his big wooden throne. He wallops his gavel then starts talking slow and loud, tossing off a belch, then going on and on about the court and what folks can and can't do. More than once he says he'll damn well clear the court room if anybody riles him and I figure him and Granger are in cahoots on that count.

I know they're all staring at me and I feel a queer sort of pride mixed up with my fear, a dark sense of specialness. I want to look out to see if any of them might see the good in me, but Mr. Finch told me to keep still. I don't feel quite right, likely since I didn't sleep much. My head is pounding and my eyes burn. Sounds come at me like they're through a megaphone. I'm jumpy, which don't look good at all. I sit on my hands.

The judge is talking to the jury now so I turn to look up at the balcony. I can see Fat Frank and Bessie up there right by the front rail with the other black folks and I lift my hand to wave and he lifts his hand and Bessie gasps real loud and this causes folks to stir and the judge bangs his gavel.

"My wife nearly made me stay in bed today the way my head's pounding so you all best stay still. I will not tolerate nonsense," he says.

The judge and me both got bad heads so I see that as a good sign. He's as big as Fat Frank but white as chalk with a white head of hair and white eyebrows and I think he looks like a gigantic rabbit. They call him the honorable Judge Augustus Laclede.

"You want a glass of water?"

It's Finch, my lawyer. I nod and shut my eyes and think of the river and keep them shut there, under my own God's eye, them million black nights, all the times swimming , never knowing it would come to this, and I start to settle down since that's what Finch and I went over. I gotta seem right in the head, he said. That's my only chance. If I go off my rocker I'm a goner. They'll finish me up before the dinner bell.

He brings me the water from a pitcher on a table. A scrawny fellow with a notepad and a big bald-headed man wearing a white shirt and a tie are both sitting at the table. There's a bible there. I can see a flashy looking man in the front row watching me and figure he must be from the paper. The judge wallops that gavel again to get things going and I nearly jump out of my seat.

I'm still shaking and I take in a deep breath to calm down. That's when Snopes starts to laugh. A real quiet laugh. Finch has got a hand on my shoulder and I drink my water and I keep telling myself I ain't scared of him. I think of last time I saw him, the black madness in his eyes, his head face down in the water and I'm thinking maybe I shoulda held him down there a while longer, finished him off and maybe I'd gotten away and right now be laying under a swath of stars out west. He's laughing louder and I can feel his bony fingers on the back of my neck and I'm sure he's just behind me, ready to strangle the life outta me.

"Mr. Snopes, what in tarnation do you find so amusing? Mr. Vest you best manage your client's decorum better," the judge says.

I turn real quick to get another look at Snopes.

He's dressed in a fancy plaid suit, all red and black and he wears that dark red carnation in his button hole. I see the judge sizing him up like he means to land that gavel, but Snopes stops laughing. Snopes turns quick and stares straight at me and mouths something I can't make out then he puts a finger in his mouth and sucks on it and his eyes go wide and I shudder. The judge turns and gives me a good looking over and I lower my head.

"Meet his eyes," Finch whispers, giving me a pinch.

I look up. The judge gives me a long stare then sighs and looks away.

"And sit up. Don't fidget," Finch says.

It's mighty hot already and my collars soaked with sweat. I can hear the flap of the ladies' hand fans. The jury's off to my left in hardback chairs looking bored. I recognize a few of the men from town and there's one man wearing a suit with the widest lapels I ever seen.

I know each of the lawyers gets to tell what they call the truth. Mr. Vest, who looks like a dandy with his hair slicked back and his shoes spit-shined, goes first. He keeps pointing at me and telling how I planned it all, how I planned to kill Snopes, getting real lively like a stage actor and making me out like a terrible villain. He's got a powerful way of speaking and I can see the jury waking up.

Finch takes it more slow which I'm not sure is a good idea. He gets real close to the jury talking low (I figure to sound serious), but the judge yells at him to speak up. This rattles him and he forgets what he was saying and has to come back to look at his notes on the table and I can see his face is wet with sweat just like mine. He turns back to the jury and lays it out that it was self-defense pure and simple. He stands there for a little while saying nothing until the judge smacks his gavel and tells him to get on with it.

When he sits down I see his hands are shaking and I wonder if he might be a morning drinker. Overall, it's not such a good start.

*Mr. Granger. A confession.*

MR. VEST CALLS the policeman Granger to the stand. The only sound is the soft waving of the hand fans.

"You arrested the defendant on the night of July 31, correct?"

"Yes sir," Granger says.

"Can you tell us how that went?"

Granger, nearly six foot four, looks confused by the question and uncomfortable in the thin wooden chair. He takes out a handkerchief and mops his brow. "What ya mean?"

"Did he surrender easily?"

"Well no. He ran like a crazy man. Trying to catch that midnight train I figure. Can I get a glass of water? It's awful hot."

They get him the water. He gulps it down and seems revived.

"Tell us about that night."

"We'd been hunting for him and found him running across that dead stretch of land that goes to the tracks, near the river ya know. I fired a shot in the air but he ran like a jack rabbit. Lucky for me, my man Bellows was with me. He's pretty fit so he ran like fire and caught the kid. Dove for his legs and got him on the ground. Knocked him around a bit."

"Thank you," Vest says. "Running for dear life you'd say."

"Yes sir, that's right."

"And what happened once you took him to the station?"

"Like I said, he got knocked around a bit. But before he passed out he was hell bent on confession. Spit it all out like he needed us to know. Flat out told us he knocked Mr. Snopes over the head and stole his money and left him there to die."

"Thank you. No further questions."

Mr. Finch is up next. He saunters over to the witness stand, then turns and smiles at the jury.

"Did you interview the defendant the night you arrested him?" Finch says.

"No. He confessed and we had Mr. Snopes' story so that was all we needed," says Granger. "Plus, I think he was running on adrenaline. He passed out and was in a bad way at first. The doc had to look in."

I look fast over at Snopes. He's plucking petals from that red carnation he had in his button hole. All the sudden, real quick like, he takes one of the petals and sticks it in his mouth.

"Did the defendant mention that Mr. Snopes asked him to go to the cabin? Did he tell you everything that happened?"

"No, just that confession."

"He said nothing else?"

Granger leans forward and puts his hands together. His forehead scrunches up like he's thinking real hard.

"Once we got him locked up, before he fell out, before the doc came. He did yell and carry on for a spell," Granger says. "I figure it was sinking in, what he was up against. Attempting to kill a man. Assault with a deadly weapon. I think he got riled being in the cell. That happens to a man."

"Do you recall what he was carrying on about?"

"We didn't get that part down since he confessed."

"Anything at all you can remember from his rant?"

Granger scrunches his brow again. "Well, one thing, which seemed strange. After a while he quieted down a bit. Right before he went out, like I said. He came on up to the bars and kept saying 'He had a gun. He was gonna kill me. He had a gun.'"

"Did you ask him about that?"

"We didn't find no gun at that shack. Nothing but some old whip. The place was flooded."

"Was the defendant examined?"

"You mean by a doctor?"

"Yes, sir."

"Sure, once the doc came. Next day."

"And?"

"Doc said he knocked his head bad. But he turned out all right as you can see."

"Was Mr. Snopes questioned about the gun?"

"Well no, like I said the kid was just ranting."

"Was Mr. Snopes examined?"

"He seen his own doctor sure. But no, we didn't do that."

"How did he look that night?"

"Mr. Snopes?"

"Yes."

"He was wet."

"Did he have bruises, cuts, was his head bleeding?"

"I don't think so. Like I said he was soaking wet. He told us what happened then left."

Mr. Finch turns around facing the jury and looking pretty proud of himself, but I can't see that he's done much. "No further questions."

*The cook. A dangerous character?*

Mr. Vest calls a plump lady wearing a blue church bonnet and a heavy gingham dress as his next witness. I recognize her as the cook from Mrs. Brattridge's party. Muttering, she lumbers up. The bald man from the table has her swear on the bible before she settles down with a thump in the chair by the judge.

"Lord it's hot," she says real loud. "And I make my living by a stove!"

The crowd titters and the judge smiles.

Mr. Vest saunters up. "State your name."

"Mrs. Maude Sweetwater."

"You are the main kitchen cook at the home of Mr. Charles Brattridge."

"Yes, I am, sir, and grateful every day for that," she says, then points into the crowd. "And the dearest lady I ever know, Mrs. Brattridge, such a fine lady to—"

The judge don't smack his gavel but he cuts her off.

"Mrs. Sweetwater, just answer the questions so we can get you back to what you do best," he says, smiling. "Since I know for a fact you make the best brandy bread pudding in Missouri."

He says this to her like they was old friends, which seems funny to me, but being the judge, I guess he can do as he pleases.

"Aww, now I don't know about that," she says.

Mr. Vest swings around to face the jury. "Mrs. Sweetwater, I want to take you back to a party this July at the Brattridge home."

Mrs. Sweetwater all the sudden pulls out a big blue fan from the many folds of her gingham dress and sets to cooling herself. "I don't know how you sit up there in those robes all day, Judge Laclede," she says. "It's criminal."

The judge smiles. Vest looks a bit rattled.

"You were running the kitchen at the party. Do you recognize the defendant as one of the employees that night?"

"Sure, as Saint Helen I do. He done run off and quit. Stole a bottle of wine, too, I'm sure of it."

"Objection," Finch says, standing fast but wobbling on his feet.

"Sustained. Let's stick to the facts."

Vest nods. "So, the defendant ran out on the job?"

She stops her fanning, closes it up and points it straight at me.

"I knew the minute they brought him in he knew nothing about service. We was short staffed and a few was brought on last minute but that one, he ran out scared as a rat before an hour was up."

"Is there anything else you remember about him?" Vest says.

"Excuse me for saying it, but his pants was too tight. A scandal. I think he's what they call a river boy."

The judge clears his throat then hacks a wad into a handkerchief.

"You get elderberry for that cough mixed with a thimble of whiskey," she says.

Mr. Vest moves closer to her. "One more question. Would you consider the witness a dangerous character?"

"Objection, leading the witness."

"Sustained. Thank you, Mrs. Sweetwater. Finch?"

Mr. Finch stands and puts both his hands on our table leaning forward like he's got something important to say. Then he sighs. "No questions your honor."

*Floozy in court. That night at the bar. A brawl.*

The minute I see the floozy take the stand I get a mean chill. She's got frizzy hair piled up and a lot of red on her cheeks and she's got on gloves all lady like, but her dress is low cut and cheap. The ladies in the audience whisper in low voices and the men smile and clear their throats. She'd been singing her tarty torch songs the night Clement and I went to fists. Finch goes pale. He don't look happy. I never told him about the fight. He looks like he wants to wallop me.

"I don't recall this witness on the list," Finch says.

"It was added late, check your papers sir," Vest says.

Finch sits.

"State your name, Miss," Vest says.

She sits up real tall pushing out her mighty chest and smiling like they was fixing to take her photograph. "Pearl Rose featured entertainer at the Hatch amongst other spots including New York City and—"

"Just your name, Miss Rose. Do you recognize the defendant?" asks Vest.

Putting her gloved finger to her fat lips and pouting like some wind-up doll she winks at the crowd.

"Why I recognize quite a few of the gentlemen here today."

The Judge picks up his gavel. "Miss Rose, just answer the questions. This is not a saloon but a court room."

Turning toward the Judge, pressing both hands to her bosom she gives him a look I'd call nothing less than dirty. "I am at your service, Judge Laclede," she says.

"Miss Rose..." Vest begins.

She turns to him, sighs, and gets louder. "Yeah, yeah sure I seen him in the bar. How could I ever forget that night, what a mess we had to clean up after them two finished up. And interrupting my performance like that. I was doing one of my best numbers, 'Old Bill'—they love that one," she says.

"What happened, Miss Rose?"

"Call me Pearl, honey."

The crowd titters and the Judge slams his gavel. Then she turns her big doll eyes on me.

"That one was in the corner," she says pointing right at me. "Then that other one came in."

She stands up to get a look at Clement.

"Sit down," says the Judge.

"Do you mean Mr. Clement Cartwright?"

"Yeah, that one. The one that built the new building,"

"The Landsworth building."

"Yeah. I'd of gone to that party, but I had to work. A girl's gotta make a living."

The crowd titters again and this makes her happy like she's found the audience she was born for. She sits up real straight again, smiling with every tooth she has.

"Tell us what happened that night."

"Like I said I was singing my best song—'Old Bill,' it's a hoot—when them two start going at it."

"Fighting?"

"Yeah fighting. They was sitting together in the back. Everybody noticed since they ain't really suited to be friendly. I was just hitting the best part—do you know the song?"

"No."

"Well, it gets real dramatic. The guys eat it up. So, I'm getting to that part when the kid, McBride, he wallops the other guy. Just smacks him flat in the nose."

"Could you hear what they were saying?" Vest says, turning to face the crowd.

"One minute they was huddled up talking the next thing McBride punches him. Then the two start tangling," she says. "Then something real strange happened."

"Yes?"

"Well I done gave up on my number, everybody was watching the fight. And that's when McBride, he all the sudden just lays on the floor.

Right at the other one's feet. Just lays there like somebody knocked him down."

"Did Mr. Cartwright hit him?"

"Well sure, they were fighting. But that ain't why McBride stopped. It's like all the sudden he just gave up and lay down at Cartwright's feet. It was something else. Then he grabbed him around the legs and started wailing."

"He was crying?"

"Yeah, holding onto the man's legs and crying. It was the oddest fight I ever seen," she says.

At this line, she lifts her face up to the balcony, like she's playing the crowd and smiles real broad. "And I tell ya I seen em all!"

"Would you say the defendant is a violent man?"

Mr. Finch hops up with his objection and the Judge agrees.

"No further questions."

"That's it?" she asks.

"Your witness, Mr. Finch."

Mr. Finch has hunched into himself like he's getting ready to fold over a few more times and disappear. That old tart's testimony set us back bad. "No questions."

I'm feeling pretty low, being as here's the second witness Finch ain't even talked to. I'm thinking I'm doomed, then looking back behind me, I see Clement. He's staring right at me from the third row and his eyes are clear and he lifts his hand like we was far away, alone at the river, and he was calling me over. And just behind him is a grand lady in a black brocade dress wearing a hat with a veil and she starts to lift the veil and I see the kindest face there, Mrs. Brattridge, who was so good to me coming to the jail. She's like an angel come to watch over me and for a second, I think things are gonna be all right, that she's gonna reach out to me and come close with that hushing voice of hers. Then the judge bangs his gavel and things keep moving.

*Pretty Boy Pete.*

PRETTY BOY PETE'S being sworn in. He's wearing real tight green pants, a dirty white shirt open low and a red silk scarf. He's the nastiest river boy I ever met, mean as a hornet. He's small and tight-muscled and struts like a rooster. He's just a tad over five-foot-tall, but strong enough to hoist a fella twice his size into the river (that I seen with my own eyes). I figure somebody musta paid him to come here to try to muddy my name. Pete don't do nothing for free, but he'll do damn near anything for a dollar. Everybody on the river knows the story about Pete and what he did with that horse.

He gets in the witness chair and smirks at me, showing off his fancy gold front tooth, then he slides down in the chair a bit and spreads his legs wide open, stretching. Pete and I had one good fuck that first year I was living on the river. I figure he's reminding me of what he's got, though nobody who felt a piece of that needs a reminder. He's mean, like I said, but mighty good at his trade.

"Son, sit up in your chair," says the judge.

Pete sits up a bit, smiling wide, gold flashing.

"Mr. Mandell," Vest says.

"Call me Pete."

"Do you recognize the defendant?"

"Sure do," Pete says. "We both work the river."

"Would you call him a trustworthy man?"

"Hell no," Pete says. "He'd steal your wallet then help you find it."

Finch hops up objecting and the judge goes our way.

"Would you consider him a violent man, based on your personal interactions with the defendant?"

Pete puts his hands on his thighs and leans forward. "We tangled a few times. Once he knocked me out so hard I hit my head and when I woke up my granpappy's gold pocket watch was gone."

Finch leans over to me. "That true?"

"We fought. I never stole no watch."

"Did the defendant tell you about his plans to go west?" Vest says.

"He told anybody that'd listen. He kept saying a few more dollars and I'm on my way. He always said he'd do anything to get west. Anything." Pete looks right at me. "I always wished I coulda taken him up on that dare."

"No further questions. Your witness, Mr. Finch."

Mr. Finch takes his time standing up, but he stays at our table.

"Have you ever robbed a man?" Finch says.

Pete laughs out loud, then runs one hand across his chest smiling. "I gotta answer that, Judge?"

"Yes."

"Well sure. Like I said we live on the river."

Finch still don't move. Just stands next to me. "Do you get in a lot of fights?"

"Sure."

"How often do you get drunk?"

Pete snorts and laughs real loud. "I sure could use one now!"

The crowd titters a bit but the judge don't raise his gavel.

"Do you drink every night?"

"Sure, don't everybody?"

"Were you drunk the night you claim the defendant stole your watch?"

"What watch?"

Finch pauses for effect.

"Oh yeah, grandpappy's watch! Drunk? Most likely. I can't remember that far back. I barely remember what I ate for breakfast."

"But you were pretty certain he stole your watch?"

"Well I figured sure. I guess. Hell, I don't know."

"No further questions."

And Finch takes his seat. Finally, he done something good.

*Snopes takes the stand.*

WHEN THEY CALL Snopes up to the stand the courtroom goes quiet. I can hear Snopes humming to himself as he saunters slowly to the witness chair. He turns and faces the crowd, bearing that crazy fanged smile.

"You solemnly swear to tell the truth and nothing but the truth."

Snopes eyes go wide and he looks at the bible like he never seen it before. Then he moves to his chair.

"Mr. Snopes, put your hand on the bible and take the oath," Judge Laclede says.

"Why? I am a soothsayer, a truth teller. We Snopes are—"

The judge speaks loud and clear, "Sir, in this court room I am in charge. You will put you right hand on the bible and swear to tell the truth so help you God and then we will hear your testimony. Mr. Vest, did I not make myself clear? I won't put up with any malarkey!"

Before Vest can get up, Snopes turns and lifts his right hand. He's wearing white leather gloves, which is queer in the heat. He curls his lips into a grin then slowly lowers his hand, like it was moving toward a burning flame, onto the good book.

"I do."

Finally, he sits. He folds them gloved hands together. He jerks his head a little to one side, like he's got a nervous tick. He's got that wild-eyed look like he did the night at the shack. Vest stands just near Snopes' chair, facing the crowd.

"Mr. Snopes, do you see the person that assaulted you, stole your money and left you to die on the night of July 31?"

Snopes stops twining those white gloved fingers together and points at me.

"The villain sits there, the vicious and worthless——"

The judge whacks the gavel. "Mr. Vest, approach please."

Them two huddle, Judge Laclede pointing at Snopes a few times. Vest steps out.

"Mr. Snopes, please try to stick with yes and no answers. We have your sworn testimony that the defendant lured you to the shack in question under false pretenses. Is that right?"

"Yes."

"He bludgeoned you, stole your money and left you in the flooding shack."

"Yes, that's right."

"Thank you," Vest says. "Your witness."

I'm awful worried about Mr. Finch. He's fussing with his pocket watch and when he grabs a water glass to take a drink his hand shakes and he spills it. I think he's surprised Vest asked so few questions.

"Mr. Finch?" says the judge.

Finch gets up and stands by his chair. Finch's got a long strand of gray hair standing straight up on the back of his head. Looks like he slept on it wrong. Snopes keeps his eyes on the jury, not giving Finch no mind at all. I try to remember any kind of prayer I mighta heard years back. Nothing comes to me so I just whisper, "Help me, Lord."

"Mr. Snopes," Finch says.

Snopes don't answer and don't look away from the jury. Finch walks over and stands in front of the jury, getting Snopes' eye, which I think is smart.

"Good morning sir," Finch says.

Snopes don't say a thing.

Finch smiles. "You testified that the accused lured you to the shack by the river. That he hit you over the head, stole your money, and left you to die, is that correct?"

Snopes stays still. I look up to the courthouse dome, to see if that white bird is still there. I can't see it.

"Answer the question, Mr. Snopes," Judge Laclede says.

"Yes."

Finch takes out a handkerchief and wipes his forehead. Then he turns and faces the jury. "The fact is you own that shack isn't that right?"

"I own and rent a lot of property. I do not keep track of all that," Snopes says. "I was not aware it was my property at the time."

"Do you consider yourself a smart man, Mr. Snopes?"

This catches Snopes' attention. He leans forward in his chair. "We Snopes are known for our brilliance."

Finch turns and walks toward him. "You run a very successful business, is that correct?"

"Yes. My family brewery. That's common knowledge."

"As you said, you own a lot of property, correct?"

At this Mr. Vest hops up to object but the judge hushes him. "You best make a point, Mr. Finch," he says.

"What I am getting at here, Mr. Snopes, is you aren't the type of man to be so easily duped," Finch says. "To be taken in by an uneducated orphan."

I sit up straight. Ain't nobody called me an orphan for a long time. I figure he's trying for sympathy.

"I at times can be too kind. I was taken in by the wretch. I thought he was in dire straits."

"And what exactly did this stranger, this servant, say to you that was so compelling that you agreed to leave an important party and go to an unknown river shack, alone with him?" Finch says. "It must have been quite a story!"

"I'm tired of these questions," Snopes says, standing.

"Sit down, Mr. Snopes," the judge says, louder than normal and looking a bit riled. "Answer the questions as they are asked."

Snopes turns and faces Laclede. That big white-haired judge don't look like he ruffles easily.

"Would you like me to repeat the question, Mr. Snopes?" Finch says.

As Snopes turns back to face the crowd to sit, I see something I remember from the night in the shack. There's a fiery look in his eyes, a rising of his scrawny shoulders like he's gonna sprout wings and spit flames.

"He said a friend of his was in a terrible state and needed help. He pleaded with me. I was drawn in," Snopes says, each word coming out slow and steady. "I confess to a moment of pity. We Snopes are human, too, you know, though we have through history been deified."

Snopes begins to laugh softly. The judge sighs real loud and Finch turns, hitches his thumbs in his vest and walks real easy like over to the jury box. The men there are watching him close. Finch is talking to Snopes but staring straight at the jury, which looks peculiar to me.

"Did you tell anyone you were leaving?"

"No."

"Did it cross your mind to ask someone to go with you?"

"No."

"You must have been very frightened, going alone with this dangerous young man," Finch says looking out at the crowd. "He's quite a bit sturdier than you."

The jury sizes up first me, then Snopes.

"Nothing frightens a Snopes," Snopes says. "He's a bit of nothing that one, harmless."

At this the crowd titters and that old judge takes notice, sitting forward.

"Harmless?" Finch says turning back to Snopes. "You testified that you feared for your life. That it was a brutal attack."

Snopes brings a gloved finger to his lips.

"Which is it? Harmless or brutal?" Finch says.

"But there is one thing you don't you know. He did not act alone," Snopes says.

"Someone else was there?"

"Yes."

The judge leans forward listening but frowning.

"Please tell us who." Finch says.

"Clement Cartwright."

There is a rush of voices, Vest gets up but the judge wallops his gavel and tells Vest to sit.

"Mr. Snopes," the judge says. "You best get your story straight."

Snopes smiles. "He was not there physically, but he infested that young man's mind. What no one knows is that young man was doing what Mr. Cartwright had told him to do. I know that for a fact. Cartwright wants me dead!"

The crowd is making noise.

"Mr. Snopes, those are wild accusations and Mr. Cartwright is not on trial here. I want to see both attorneys in my chambers," the judge says.

"I swear I can tell you how I know this," Snopes says.

"Go on," says the judge.

"I saw those two together. Cartwright and Calhoun. I followed them, I heard them. They spent nights together. They plotted. They are an unnatural pair!"

The gavel flies and the judge booms, "You can step down, Mr. Snopes. We will have a recess. You two in my chambers."

*The prosecution rests. Fever-heat. The defense calls Fat Frank.*

THE PROSECUTION RESTED and the judge gave us a recess. It's time to eat, but I can't touch the food they bring. Finch lets me smoke. I wish I could get to Clement but I can't. Noon comes and goes and the fever-heat keeps rising, topping a hundred, unsettling my thinking and bringing on a dry-mouthed dizziness. It's hard to focus on much of anything. Finch says the judge is telling the jury to ignore what Snopes said about Clement, that that part has been *stricken*, but how can anybody just forget threats like them? And thing is I know it's true. And Clement was trying to protect us from Snopes.

There's a huge hunk of ice at the foot of the courthouse steps and most folks run out to get a piece but they won't let me outta the building. I wonder if Clement went out, took some ice and ran it on his neck. Even now, all of this, and I can't stop thinking of how damn sweet it would be to get close to that spot on the side of his neck, the taste of him, all that we done. I'm a real no-good, I figure. I undone that man. Undone him. I told Finch I want to testify but he hushed me, said let's see how it goes.

We get back into court. Snopes ain't moved. I swear he never got out of his chair, sitting straight up with those white glove hands on. He don't seem to sweat either.

"You ready?" Finch says. "It's our turn."

I nod, thinking it don't matter two shits if I'm ready or not. They call Fat Frank. It takes a while for him to get down from the balcony. Folks are buzzing too, him being who he is and all. Standing up there, near that big white-haired judge and the bald fella at the front table, Fat Frank looks mighty regal to me. It's not just his being tall or wide, there's something in the way he keeps his back straight, gently puts his big old hand on the bible, moves and sits on the chair like he was at one of Mrs. Brattridge's fancy dinners. He's wearing a tweed suit, the only one he owns which must feel pretty miserable in the heat. He takes a minute to look down and get my eye before they start and it feels like he's next to me, us two by the river at night, laughing, him putting an arm across my shoulder.

"State your name," says Finch.

"Franklin Carmel Leary."

"Do you know the defendant?"

"Yes, I do, sir."

"How do you know him?"

"He lived with me for a spell."

"What is your relationship?"

Frank turns and smiles at me. "He's the best friend I ever had. And the best man I ever knowed."

I can't see for a minute. He's a blur up there and I can't catch my breath 'cause I need to say something to him and I can't.

"You have heard the charges against the defendant. Can you still call him a good man?"

Frank stays real still. He turns to look at the jury, two lines of white men who don't seem so interested.

"Calhoun's heart is pure. He'd never hurt nobody but to save his own life. He don't have a lick of bad in him."

"Thank you, Mr. Leary. Your witness."

Vest gets up fast, like he was chomping at the line. "Have you ever been incarcerated? That word means 'imprisoned,' Mr. Leary. As in jailed?"

Frank lowers his head.

"It's public record. Ten years for assault. Back in Louisiana," Vest says.

"I done my penance."

"So, by your standard the defendant is a fine young man. I see. You have an interesting taste in friends, Mr. Leary. What is your relationship with Bessie Stash?"

"She's a friend."

"A friend? You do keep fine company. Miss Stash has been arrested for solicitation plus the fact is Miss Stash is not—"

All the sudden Frank stands up. He don't move but he stands and speaks slow and steady, "Don't bring her into this."

"Sit down," the judge says.

"Don't bring her up or you might do what? Maybe knock me out and take my money? Like your friend there."

Finch objects and Vest withdraws.

"You may step down."

Vest stays quiet but Frank don't move.

"You're done, Mr. Leary," the judge says.

Frank looks up and I see what he's feeling, I see him taking it all on, like he was gonna tell them how good I am and it was gonna set me free. I see in the long sorrow of that face that he really believed he could make a difference. He gets up and I can't stop myself. I jump up as he's passing me.

"You done good, Frank," I yell.

The judge hits the gavel and Finch settles me down, then I turn and watch as Frank makes his way down the long center aisle, out and away, up to the balcony.

*A fine lady in a veil.*

Mr. Finch calls up Mrs. Brattridge. He told me that her being a fine lady, a few kind words might go a long way with the jury. She moves past me, all in mourning black, even that hat and veil. She lifts the veil to be sworn in and I see how pretty she is, how fine she looks after all the riffraff that come up before her. Finch goes to her side.

"Thank you for coming today having lost your husband, Ma'am," he says. "I am truly sorry."

She nods.

"Do you know the defendant?"

"Yes," she says in a near whisper.

The judge leans forward. "Ma'am, I too gotta say how sorry I am for your loss. I ask both of you gentlemen to keep this brief. I do have to ask you to speak up so the jury can hear you."

The jury is watching her real close, and I figure a lot of them ain't used to seeing her type.

"How do you know the defendant?" Finch asks.

"I learned of his case and went to see him. I knew right away he was a gentle young man."

Vest hops up. "Objection."

"Overruled. I will allow it," says the judge turning to the jury. "The jury understands these are Mrs. Brattridge's opinions. But I would like to know her impressions."

"You saw him in jail?" Finch says. "That's mighty kind of you."

"Yes. I spoke to him," she says. "I spent time with him. I felt I knew him."

For a moment she seems lost. She lowers her head. Then she looks up and stares right at me. "I do know him. I know he is a good person. I can sense that, you see. No matter what he has done, in his heart he is good."

"Thank you, Ma'am. Your witness."

Vest approaches her. "I too am sorry for your loss, Ma'am. And I know you have not been well, not well at all."

"I'm fine."

"Of course, considering. I'll keep this brief with the heat, and your history of fainting."

"I'm perfectly well now, sir," she says.

"I'm sure, Ma'am, though your doctor must be concerned. He prescribes you laudanum, am I right?"

She looks out into the crowd but does not answer.

"Ma'am?" Vest says.

"Yes. For sleeping."

"For sleeping?" he says. "Did you take laudanum today, Ma'am?"

Finch stands. "Is this necessary?"

"I'd like to know the mental state of the witness," Vest says.

"I'll allow it," the judge says. "Answer the question, Ma'am. Did you take laudanum today?"

There is a pause. The court is dead-quiet.

"Yes," she says softly.

"Thank you, Ma'am, that will be all." He says.

Finch sighs real loud. Things didn't go at all like he hoped. I watch Mrs. Brattridge slowly getting up, that veil hanging over her face. It's like all the air went out of her, and it takes her a while to move past me, slow and steady, like she was still at a funeral.

Mr. Finch turns to me. "I'm calling Clement."

"No," I say.

"We're lost, son, without him. Lost."

"Then I'm telling my story, too."

He don't say nothing, just calls our next witness.

*Clement on the stand. The banging gavel.*

As CLEMENT WALKS by, I get an uneasy feeling, a gut burning that says this ain't good, I already done enough harm to that man. I grab the back of Finch's coat. "Don't do this. He don't need to be part of this."

Finch pulls away and ignores me, moving up to face Clement. "State your name and your business in St. Louis."

"Clement Cartwright. I am the architect of the Landsworth Building and am setting up an office for our firm in St. Louis. I grew up here."

"You are a St. Louis man at heart?"

Clement tugs at his collar but don't answer. He's wearing a dark suit with a tight vest and a bow tie. His hair is slicked and even from where I sit I can see sweat on his brow. The heat's coming on full force. It's a steamy day. I can't look at him without wanting to touch him.

"And how do you know the defendant?"

"I met him at the Planter's House Hotel," Clement says, looking my way.

Snopes coughs real loud but the judge don't pay him no mind. My heart's racing.

"We struck up a conversation. I knew they needed help at the bar so I asked the bartender to talk to him. He right away gave him a job. He saw he'd be a good hire."

"And what can you say about the defendant, in your dealings with him?"

Clement looks down in his lap and I don't think that's good. Mr. Finch always tells me to keep my head up and look men in the eye. Then he lifts his head and looks to the jury. "He's one of the finest, most upstanding young men I have ever met."

The crowd makes a pretty awful stir over this, and the judge goes at it with his gavel.

"A young man who has admitted to stealing and hitting a man over the head?" Finch says. "Upstanding?"

Clement keeps staring at the jury. His face is shining with sweat and now he's clenching his fists. "He's a fine young man. I won't stand by and see him wronged."

"Do you think he set out to harm Mr. Belasco Snopes on the night in question?" Finch says.

"No. He was defending himself."

"Thank you, sir. Your witness."

Vest moves in fast. "You seem to have taken a real interest in the defendant. Getting him a job out of the kindness of your heart? Calling him a fine young man even though we heard testimony that the two of you brawled at a tavern. You mustn't hold a grudge."

"I had too much to drink that night, that's all."

"How often did you see the defendant once you got him that job?"

"Just a few times."

"Really? What about in your hotel room?"

Clement says nothing.

Vest turns to the jury. "Well, let me remind you, sir. The defendant spent the night in your hotel room on at least seven nights this past month. I have several eye witnesses."

Finch is up. "Objection. Mr. Cartwright is not on trial here."

"I'll allow it. You brought on a character witness. We need to know his character. Continue, Mr. Vest."

Clement is sitting up real straight, his shoulders thrust back like he's going to battle. His fists are clenched and resting on the sides of the chair. Vest is standing close to him, looking first at Clement, then at the jury as he talks. He's got a real smug look on his face which makes me nervous.

"Let me try to understand this: Here's a young man that lives on the river and who is known to associate with dangerous types. And you invite him to spend the night with you? Seems mighty strange to me."

Vest turns to the jury shrugging his shoulders like he's confused.

"He needed a place to stay. We all fall on hard times."

"How kind of you!"

Vest says it in a way that makes it clear he don't believe Clement. He hitches his thumbs in his suspenders which are under his jacket and walks toward the jury. Clement is still sitting up real stiff in his chair.

"Are you married, sir?"

"No, I am not."

"Do you have a lady friend?" Vest winks at Clement which riles him. He lifts his hands from the sides of the chair like he's fixing to punch Vest, then he lowers his hands again, and looks down.

"No."

"Now that room you were in had but one bed. Did the kid sleep on the floor?"

*Stricken testimony.*

"Tread lightly, Mr. Vest," the judge says. "Move this along."

Vest smiles, turns to the jury. "Mr. Cartwright, do you like Belasco Snopes?"

Clement grimaces, which don't seem like the best thing to do. "You don't need to like everyone you do business with."

"Mr. Snopes has testified that——"

"Mr. Vest, don't try my patience. That testimony was stricken," the judge says.

Mr. Vest purses his lips. He turns back to Clement. "Do you believe Mr. Snopes' story about the night in question?"

"I do not."

"But why not? Why would you not believe your business partner over this destitute young man?"

Clement looks my way, and I see him clenching his fists again and his cheeks go scarlet. I grab Mr. Finch's arm real tight and I know we gotta stop this but it's too late.

"There is nothing but evil in Belasco Snopes. He is hell bent on ruining me and he is using this young man to do it. He is a liar and a murderer and I know that for a fact!"

There's suddenly so much going on that I can hardly focus. The judge is pounding his gavel but Clement won't shut up. The crowd is making a ruckus and Snopes is on his feet yelling.

"I know Snopes killed the prostitute Jenny Claire," Clement says. "He is the villain here."

The uproar is as loud as the river raging. Men are shouting, and one woman faints.

Snopes has moved out into the aisle. "Shut him up. Cut out his tongue, the dirty drab!"

"Snopes is a tyrant! Go to his brewery and you will find her remains. I know what he is! I have always known!" Clement's face looks to be burning. "It's all lies!"

The judge, the lawyers, half the court is up and shouting and moving around but who I notice most is Snopes himself, who has lifted his face to the sky, lifted his arms over his head and is laughing out loud. He won't stop laughing. He won't stop.

*The final witness.*

Judge Laclede told the whole damn courtroom that if there was one more outburst he'd clear every last person out. He had a long talk with both lawyers, too. Then we had a break. I made it clear to Finch during the break that I was gonna testify, and he finally gave in saying "it's your hide" and I know its right being that things have gone so far to shit. After the break, everybody got seated back in court and the judge came in wiping his mouth and coughing.

"Call your witness," the judge says.

When Finch calls me to the front, I stand up and lean on the desk since my legs feel wobbly. It's quiet, though my ears are buzzing. I move up to the witness stand and I can hear the sound of my feet across the wood floor and it feels like they're too heavy to lift. They hurt in these hard city shoes Finch made me wear. They're too big, and as I step forward my foot twists and my legs buckle and I go down flat on my face. There's a gasp from the crowd, and an echo of that bird flapping way up, then Snopes starts making a dark, growling noise that crawls straight up my back. It's like a laugh, but coming from somewhere deep in his throat. Finch is helping me up to the stand.

"Mr. Finch, is your client sickly?" Judge Laclede says.

"Just nerves, your honor. He's fine."

I make it up there and get sworn in and am glad to sit. My head is pounding something awful and I'm sweating.

"Why don't you tell us what happened the night in question…"

I sit up a little straighter in the hard-backed witness chair. I can see the whole crowd. Rows and rows of faces staring, and up above the black faces looking down. It's like the whole town showed up. I ain't never been looked at so hard in my life. I spot Clement. His face is still as a stone. He looks scared to death.

"Take you time," Finch says.

The courtroom is still, only the soft sound of people's fans in the heat.

"I was working," I say.

All the sudden Finch starts coughing, like he's gonna hack up a lung. He goes over and drinks his water then comes back. "Throat's dry," he says. "Now, you were working at the Landsworth party?"

"Yes," I say.

"And that's when you spoke to Mr. Snopes?"

"He asked me to fetch him a drink. That was my job. Then he asked me to go with him."

"Go with him where?"

"To his shack."

There is a rising wave of voices, and the judge pounds his gavel. Folks quiet down and I look out toward Clement but Snopes has got me, them black eyes cutting into me and I look away.

"What happened next?" Finch says.

"He said he'd pay me forty dollars if I left with him."

More gasping, that gavel.

"And you said yes?"

"That's a lot of money," I say.

"So, you went with him,"

"He took me to his cabin."

Finch keeps asking questions and the crowd makes noise and that gavel goes up and down. I tell how we went to the cabin and how the rain poured. I keep talking 'cause I know I gotta tell the worst of it. I tear my eyes away from Snopes and look straight up at the huge dome ceiling above us all and focus on the light up there but it don't work, the more questions he asks the more I see the cabin, the water rising, the blood on the floor, and me getting on all fours. We're up to that part in the story and he wants me to tell it and I look down at the floor and think I might pass out but I know I gotta tell it. And they all gonna think I'm crazy.

"He told me to get on all fours," I say.

There is gasping but Finch charges on. I can see it all now, my face dripping sweat, Snopes on my back in the dark, riding me.

"Like a dog?" he asks.

"A horse. He told me to neigh like a horse. He rode me."

I can feel Snopes on me like it was that night and the court goes black in my head so I rub my eyes. I'm hot and dizzy and Finch asks what I mean by a horse. Mr. Vest stands up shouting but Finch shouts louder and the judge tells them both to simmer down and tells me to carry on and I look out and it's like Snopes flew forward, like he grew wings and was right in my face breathing fire on me and bouncing on my back and I can feel the water on my ankles, the river running red, and feel his hands on my shoulders and he's standing up at his table and I think they gotta know how it really was that night, I gotta save myself. So, I stand up fast an make a loud neighing sound, over and over, shutting my eyes and tossing my head back so they all can see what happened. My throat gushes with sound and my whole body shakes and the gavel pounds harder right against my skull and Snopes pulls out a gun, screaming, pointing it, just like that night, screaming he'll kill me.

I see Clement running up toward me, shielding me then I hear the crack, a shot. Clement falls. Blackness takes over and I pass out.

# PART FIVE

# FORTY-SIX

*Belinda's message. A new girl.*

*Belasco Snopes*

THE SEA IS tumultuous and there is a bashing of waves, and more softly, a pale calling that no one hears but me, a dark screaming of souls lost to a blue and icy death, pierced by the sea's force and forever staining the water red.

Most of the travelers are huddled sick in their cabins as our captain steers the mighty Mauretania steamer through this late summer tempest chugging its way to Italy.

The ship's dining room is empty. I've chosen potted shrimps, mutton chops, boiled capon and cold rolled ox tongue. The feast is spread before me. A mad man's supper?

"You will plead temporary insanity propelled by the false defamation of your character," my lawyer insisted. "You were aiming the gun wildly and it went off by accident. You had no malicious intent. We will dissolve the charges against McBride and you will take a long leave."

Temporary insanity. If only they knew. My intention was exact and I would do it again, indeed I may find my way to Chicago someday, may set right this injustice by putting a bullet in Cartwright's addled brain. But not now.

I shove a shrimp in my mouth and swallow it whole knowing I have delivered my blood to the two-faced scoundrels of St. Louis, men whose lives I propped up higher than they could ever have done on their own. Sniveling cowards. Daddy is surely howling in his grave.

Our St. Louis, Snopes' kingdom. All we did to grow that sniveling fur trading post, over a hundred years of fine Snopes' maneuvering gone in an instant. Pulverized by a two-bit delinquent and a deviant architect. My glory tossed to the sea and shunned. "You must leave St. Louis," my lawyer said.

I wash my hands of the lot of them. I will not give them what they could have had; I will not give them the best of me. Their puny minds can never imagine, will never grasp their loss. Perhaps I shall travel past Italy to the wilds of Africa, find a voodoo witch to send a plague of curses to that city, and then to Cartwright.

Belinda enters this massive, ghostly dining room, a vision in frothy crimson silk. She approaches slowly, but not with trepidation. The black mahogany dining tables are paired with overstuffed club chairs. The cream silk covering the chairs is embroidered with vines and exotic flowers, recalling that ghastly jungle of Mrs. Brattridge.

Above me, the restaurant's domed ceiling is glass, offering a view to the bleak sky and the storm's onslaught. Belinda is facing me and I have to admit she is a lovely girl. How long before the fresh pluck of youth will fade, before marriage, child rearing and living the life of a German beer barren's wife will smear that rosiness away. But for now, she is useful. Her good standing in society, her reputation, helped soften the rising outrage against me after the trial. The accusations were outlandish, and our lawyer took it all in hand. Still, he suggested we move her wedding to Italy, and that I stay away from St. Louis for a "good long while" as he put it.

Belinda asks the waiter for champagne before I can tell him what to bring her.

"You're not eating?" I say, stabbing my ox tongue.

"Heinrich warned me about the trials of a journey at sea and suggested I fast which I'm grateful for."

There is something odd about her. She is looking at me too directly, too boldly.

I clear my throat. "Do you know how they dislodge the ox tongue? They take the animal and—"

"Did you kill the girl?" she asks.

I look at her. With her skin like alabaster, it has always been easy to see those lips tremble. Those lips, however, do not tremble now.

"Do you know what Daddy did in the brewery late at night?" I say.

She stands up abruptly and her crimson silk billows and she does not look away. "I don't care, Belasco."

I chuckle with amusement at her outburst.

"Did you do it?"

"The prostitute?" I ask. "Is that the girl you are referring to?"

"Are there others?" she asks.

"Sit down and eat something. You look terrible."

She does not move. Her lips move but I do not hear anything over a sudden burst of hail battering the glass dome above us. "I will not allow you near my children," she says.

She looks at me and I see familiar disgust but there is something more. The look of terror is gone and there is steeliness in its place.

"You are pregnant, aren't you?" I say. "That's the change."

"What did father do you to you?" she says quietly.

I stab the mutton and place a slab in my mouth. "Did you know human bones are dense and difficult to crush? It takes a great deal of patience. It can take all night," I say. "But once crushed they can be scattered in corners, into dirt or tossed into vats of beer. And then it is as if the person never existed."

I look up from my plate to watch her leave, her narrow elegant back, the pile of hair, the soft noise of her heeled shoe the only sound other than the rain. I finish the chop then wave the waiter over to ask for dessert.

A plain looking girl has entered the dining room, moving slowly. She is a tiny thing, like a fragile bird dressed in bright yellow, one hand at her tiny mouth, as if indicating the need for food. I stand and she sees me, hesitates, and then walks through the empty dining room toward my table. I attempt a smile. It will be important to find a wife, to bear a son, a Snopes heir. I will not allow Belinda to rob me on that front.

It will, of course, be necessary to deal smartly with my sister, but first this unexpected bit stepping into my web, moving closer, closer toward me as the ship sways and she lowers her hand to her tiny waist then smiles and opens her mouth to speak.

# FORTY-SEVEN

*Convalescing in the garden.*

*Dolores Brattridge*

THE SUN IS warm in my garden and they have left me dozing but I do not dream. I have lost track of time. I have been convalescing a few weeks since that terrible trial. I do not feel I had much of an effect on that whole affair, but I am happy the young man, Calhoun, is free. I am not ill, but Edna insists I rest.

Things have settled down and with that calm--a sudden normality— my grief over losing Charles has begun to crystalize and, at times, threaten to overwhelm me. In my mind, I no longer can hear his voice, and that disturbs me greatly. Each night, I lie in the dark and try to imagine his calling to me to remove a cuff link, to tell me of things inconsequential and dull, to listen to the constant roar of his snoring. I cannot imagine the timbre of his voice. Each time I try there is nothing but an echo, a soft rush of nothingness like a constant wash of waves. It is maddening and I am recognizing what it truly means to be alone. I dream of our lost child, of Calhoun, of Charles.

It is an exceptional day, and though summer wanes, my blooms are strong, stalks swaying, vines hearty, violets, crimsons and blues shimmering like the sun-bleached sea. I shut my eyes and take in the scents, and hear a rustling, past the foliage, more a rustling of movement, of someone approaching and I keep my eyes shut thinking yes, oh yes Charles, return to me as a phantom, or is it Calhoun come back or even that Mediterranean youth I shunned so long ago. I open my eyes, turn to the separating vines, relieved. It is, of course, my deepest connection, walking to me swiftly and with direction, my dearest and forever, my Edna.

# FORTY-EIGHT

*Back on the Memphis Belle.*

"YOU'RE THE ONE involved in that trial."

I'm standing on the deck of the Mississippi Belle heading back to Chicago. I was hoping to have some time alone. A young man in black tie, part of a wedding party on the boat, has discovered me. He lights a cigar and leans on the rail next to me.

"I read about it in the paper. Damnedest thing. That Snopes sure is crazy as a loon."

"Yes," I say.

This sets the fellow laughing and he smacks me on the back.

"And you put up that new building," he says. "That's impressive."

I take another step away then turn to the fellow. He's handsome with a pencil thin mustache and hair the color of wheat. He's not much older than Calhoun.

"If you don't mind, I came out here to be alone," I say.

He backs up, puffing his cigar and grinning.

"Oh sure. Sure. It's just I read about you in the paper. Come down to the lower level and have a drink with us. We'll be at it a while."

He leaves and I return to looking at the muddy waves, relentless and restless. I didn't expect Calhoun to show up on the dock, but I had hoped. I had no idea how I'd fit him into my life back into Chicago but I didn't care, still don't care. If he ever does show up, if he has enough of his idyllic west and comes to me, I'll be ready. Or maybe I'll go find him.

Something has changed irrevocably this summer. There is no turning back for me. I lit a lost corner of myself and I will not extinguish it now. I look toward the shore, recalling the night I arrived in St. Louis, when I saw a young man waving from the river's edge. Could that have been Calhoun? Across the dark waves of the Mississippi, that same shore is empty now. Still, I can imagine him standing there. I can draw that memory close.

# FORTY-NINE

*A farewell. A palm of gold. The 9:30 train.*

*Calhoun McBride*

MISSISSIPPI RIVER AT night, mean and ain't quiet.

There's a howling in the wind and it sounds like the little ones on that Orphan Train, them crying, screaming ones begging for a place to land. But it ain't them, it ain't them ones from a time that seems so long ago. It's just the old 8:10 freight train passing. My train don't come until 9:30. A train heading west.

A wide shadow cuts across dusk down by river's edge and that's Fat Frank's making his way up to where I'm sitting, whistling some old song like he always does. I think of how his face looked during the trial, on the stand and up in that balcony, all them black faces and his so sad, so scared. I ain't never seen Fat Frank look like that. I hope he never looks like that again.

"What's good?" He finds his way to my side and hands me a bottle.

The 8:10 whistles again and I take a slug. I can barely look at him 'cause I keep thinking once I do I'll know it's one of the last times I'm gonna see them eyes, that wobbly chin, the way one tooth on the right looks all black against the other white ones when he laughs. I just keep staring at the river. We sit quiet for a few minutes.

"You ready to go?" Frank says.

I look at him. "Clement asked me to go with him."

"Yeah," he says, taking a snort.

"He sent me a note. Told me where to meet him. He got the steamer back to Illinois. Said we'd work something out."

"All right," Frank says. "So, why didn't you go with him?"

There's a stillness to the water tonight I don't recognize. It's like whatever sets it on edge, that underbelly of the river, that meanness, just shut down and went quiet.

"And do what?" I say. "Work in his kitchen? Fix his car? I sure couldn't run around with the folks he sees out there. They say he's downright famous in Chicago."

"All right," Frank says.

"'Course I thought about it," I say. "But last night I had a dream."

"Yeah," Frank says.

"I don't think I made it up, this dream. I think somebody told me this story once but in this dream it was me."

"What you getting at?"

There's another long howl and the 8:10 heads out, that cry growing softer and softer.

"Aw forget it," I say.

"Go on."

"Well, we're on a farm. Clement and me. I'm poor and he's rich."

Fat Frank chuckles which burns me. "Sounds about right," he says.

"But then I'm on a train, not the 9:30 more like a fancy train, like a train in a foreign land. Then I sort of, well this part don't make sense. But I turn around and the train's coming back but I'm dressed up and I get off and we're in a garden, that lady—Mrs. Brattridge—her garden and we sit down."

"Then what?"

"I woke up."

We both sit quiet, passing the bottle back and forth.

"What did that dream tell ya?" he says.

"A lot of nothing."

He looks down at my beat-up suitcase. "That all you got?"

"Yeah."

He twists himself sideways, fetching something out of his pocket. "Open your hand."

He sets a gold railroad pocket watch in my palm. I ain't never seen anything so beautiful.

"Every man needs a good watch," he says.

"Where'd you get this?"

"That been in my family a long time. Don't you worry none where we got it. It's yours now. It's gonna keep you on time." Then he gets up. "I best go. Bessie's waiting."

I stand up and we stand face to face, eye to eye and then he reaches out and grabs me to him, giving me a hug so tight it takes my breath away. He holds me like that and I feel the beat of his heart, the tick of that watch, and it's all the same thing to me. I start shaking and he lets me go then turns away, walking back toward the levee.

"Wait, I ain't ready," I yell.

He don't even turn around. "Sure you are," he yells back.

And I think, yeah, I am ready. Frank's right. But then Frank's always been right.

## ABOUT THE AUTHOR

Scott Alexander Hess earned his MFA in creative writing from The New School. He blogs for *The Huffington Post* and his writing has appeared in *Genre Magazine, The Fix,* and elsewhere. Hess co-wrote *Tom in America,* an award winning short film starring Sally Kirkland and Burt Young. His novel *The Butcher's Sons* was named a *Kirkus Reviews* Best Book of 2015 and his novel *Skyscraper* was a Lambda Literary Award Finalist. Originally from St. Louis, Missouri, Hess now lives in Manhattan, New York with his husband. He teaches fiction writing at Gotham Writers in New York City.

CPSIA information can be obtained
at www.ICGtesting.com
Printed in the USA
LVHW091256161019
634392LV00001B/29/P

9 781590 217122